ANDREAS TRINSCH

Brienne – A Life for Honor

AF199300

For all those, who, like me,
have grown fond of *Brienne*.

Andreas Trinsch

A Life for Honor

A Commentary Review of the "Lady of Tarth" Storyline
including "Game of Thrones" Seasons Two through Six

... and much more.

Translated from
German into English

Illustration: Philipp-Martin Wegner / www.zeichenfuchs.de
Translation: Adriana Stein

Production and publishing: BoD - Books on Demand, Norderstedt

ISBN: 978-3-7460-1444-9

With this book I simply wish to say "thanks".

"Thanks" to George R.R. Martin who created this truly unique character of *Brienne* who casts aside all traditional stereotypes and shows us that being "different" is what makes people special.

And of course "thanks" to Gwendoline Christie who not only immortalized herself with this role but who also inspired me to write this book in the first place with her wonderful portrayal of this extraordinary woman.

WHERE TO FIND EVERYTHING

Two Important Notes in Advance:

On the one hand, this book contains Brienne's storyline up to and including Season Six. If you have managed to resist all media temptations to keep you up to date on the subject, read no further. As you know... **SPOILERS AHEAD!**

On the other hand, it is dedicated exclusively to "Show Brienne" and only refers to events and narratives which are mentioned in the TV adaption up to this point.

This is primarily aimed at the readers of George R.R. Martin's novels among you who are a little wary of the series due to numerous plot changes and who may feel that there is a lack of biographical background information on "Book Brienne".

However, it could cause a great deal of confusion, particularly for non-readers, if events from the books were mixed with events from the TV production. Books should remain books and films should remain films.

What you can expect

Up until now, I have only known this feeling from long-gone days, when my film and action heroes were Lex Barker as "Old Shatterhand", Raimund Harmstorf as the Courier of the Czar "Michael Strogoff" or the now almost forgotten Peter Marshall in the role of "Orzowei" being mercilessly hunted through the African jungle. It has been a long, long time since then. Almost exactly 40 years. I was just seven years old, an age at which this kind of expression of sympathy for an artist, no matter what genre, was perfectly normal, and which is still the case for children today.

I really did not think that it was still possible, 40 years afterward, that this long-lost childhood feeling would be awakened in me again. Yet, Gwendoline Christie, a woman for a change, managed to do just this in mid-2012, when she appeared on the scene with her sympathetic interpretation of "Brienne of Tarth".

While this previously mentioned sympathy was only limited to the character at first, I was so fascinated by the way she is embodied by the actress as the story goes on that I eventually wanted to know more about the woman who so magnificently portrays this character that has been subjected to hard tests by fate.

During my research, I found some interesting information concerning how Christie actually came to *Game of Thrones*, what she did before she became part of this series and what we can expect from her in the near future. I have included everything that seemed important and worth mentioning in the following chapter.

In addition to these background facts, this book primarily offers an entertaining commentary review of Brienne's adventurous and perilous journey through the Seven Kingdoms, illustrated with numerous original scenes from the series. A journey that started promisingly with her appointment to Renly Baratheon's Kingsguard but increasingly develops into a tour full of painful experiences over time and pushes her to her limits both mentally and physically.

The main focus here is exclusively on scenes in which Brienne plays an active or passive role or in which she is at least mentioned in one way or another by other characters. Other storylines, which do not overlap or cross over her story, are only taken into account insofar as they are relevant to her further storyline. This generally takes place with highlighted explanatory reviews.

Brienne – A Life for Honor ultimately became a book, whose title, in my opinion, best describes this character. All of her actions are determined by her unwavering loyalty and her firm efforts to always do the morally right thing, to protect her self-respect and ultimately her honor.

Hamburg, February 2017

I wrote this book without the assistance of a professional proofreader.
So, if you should find any possible errors, please feel free to keep them.

Phoenix from the Ashes

For me, *Game of Thrones*, the television adaptation produced by the US television network HBO and based on George R.R. Martin's series of fantasy novels *A Song of Ice and Fire*, is the best show currently on television. It is also officially the most successful TV series across all genres in the world with its 38 Emmy awards so far, including two consecutive awards in the "Best Drama Series" category. There are plenty of reasons for this.

The "Lady of Tarth"

One of these reasons are definitely the characters created by the author. Hardly any other story offers such a wide variety of ambivalent figures like Martin's thrilling fantasy saga.

Brienne from the island of Tarth, better known as "Brienne of Tarth", is such a complex character and, in my opinion, also one of the most tragic figures in the entire *Game of Thrones* universe due to her difficult life circumstances that she has faced since early childhood.

Even when she was still a child, Brienne's father Selwyn, the Lord of Evenfall Hall, tried to find a befitting husband for his only daughter and heir to the House - without any measurable success.

With a remarkable body size for a growing girl and already towering over most men at a height of over six foot at an early age, as well as her lack of typical feminine charms, Brienne simply did not correspond to what young marriageable Lords envisaged as their Mrs. Right. Constantly rejected and somewhat humiliated by these suitors, she decided against the quiet and carefree but also uneventful life of a lady at court at an early stage, despite her noble lineage.

Firmly determined to fulfil her lifelong dream of being in the service of a Lord, who respects her as she is and treats her well and protecting him by giving her own life if necessary, she repeatedly urged her father to teach her how to wield a sword and ride a horse.

Lessons which ultimately paid off. For despite the fact that she is a woman and therefore being underestimated more often than she would like, Brienne is among the best in her field when handling a sword, and those who enjoy her trust can count themselves lucky. Aside from the fact that she is a capable and, if necessary, merciless warrior, there is hardly a more reliable and more loyal soul than her throughout Westeros. This was a realization that Renly Baratheon also came to early on.

Indeed, in the course of events, Brienne had one or two opportunities to demonstrate her abilities, however, her opponents were often no longer able to testify to her talent afterwards. Or Brienne's triumph was put down to unfortunate circumstances rather than her ability.

In fact, why does Jaime Lannister always come to my mind in this respect?

An extraordinary woman

Brienne's androgynous appearance in combination with her short, flaxen and shaggy hair, as well as the fact that she normally wears half-armor and a reinforced tunic due to her chosen life path, undoubtedly contribute to the fact that she is excluded and seen as an outsider by large sections of society; and some even have a subliminal suspicion of homosexual inclinations.

Brienne is therefore often the target of ridicule and mockery from both men and women and to describe her as "pretty" would be like describing a butcher as "vegan". It is not by chance that she has been vilified as "Brienne the Beauty" since childhood. The woman was then largely shaped by these reactions that turned her into an extremely humorless person. Since the incidents in her youth, Brienne particularly treats men with enormous distrust and often takes a snappy, demure or taciturn stance towards them. Since there was hardly anyone who had a kind word or praise for her in the past, apart from Renly Baratheon and her father, she feels rather hard-pressed in these situations and it embarrasses her to reply with thanks.

Her awkwardness in dealing with these situations can be felt in these moments, which are admittedly rare.

Even though the "Maiden of Tarth", as she is also known, is aware that can never be elevated to the status of a knight as a woman, an honor that she certainly deserves more than many actual "Sers", Brienne lives very strictly by the knight's moral code like no other character in the story, and basically applies this standard to everyone, albeit primarily to all those who have already had the fortune of being knighted. With this attitude towards life and the ultimately bitter view that it is not her qualities and skills with a sword blocking this path but simply the fact that she is the wrong gender, she has a deep contempt for anyone who breaks or takes their knightly oath lightly. Oops! There he is again, the good Jaime!

A contradictory character

Brienne's distinct sense of justice and her fundamentally honest character without falsity are certainly her outstanding characteristics, which are positive across the board, and this, even though there is hardly a character in *Game of Thrones* who is exclusively good or exclusively evil. In keeping with that, she is, in my opinion, one of the very few exceptions. While at this point it is certainly debatable whether her vengeance, which drove her on since Renly Baratheon's murder and which she ultimately took with her enforced judgement of his brother Stannis, is a positive or negative trait according to her sworn oath. Or a bit of both.

This also gives me the perfect transition to Brienne's weaknesses since they should not go unmentioned. In addition to her aforementioned lack of humor, her extreme stubbornness should also be mentioned as well as her moral principles. Yes, you read correctly. It is her almost obstinate belief in true chivalry. Really? Are virtuous actions not actually worthy of praise?

In principle, yes, but Brienne simply wears this moral corset incredibly tight. As already expressed, she follows the knight's code in such a rigorous and disciplined manner (and her stubbornness also plays a not altogether unimportant role here) that she does not even consider alternative solutions in certain situations, and it seems as if she is going through life with blinkers on. As if she can't tell her left from right. And it is precisely this stubborn clinging on to knightly principles and the associated disregard of all reason that then get her into serious difficulties. Her storyline up to now is full of examples of this.

Sure. I am going on about her weaknesses. But when a story like *Game of Thrones* releases characters such as Ramsay Bolton, Joffrey Baratheon or Petyr Baelish on the viewer, her weaknesses suddenly pale in comparison. Not to mention the fact that she compromises herself or her own mission with these weaknesses rather than other people, in contrast to the three abovementioned men. Voilà! Now that's what I call an euphemism!

If you think again about what has been written so far, Brienne's contrast between immense physicality and ruthlessness in battle, on the one hand, and internal vulnerability, on the other, will now be blatantly obvious. Like a turtle in her shell, she seems to only really feel safe in her armor. One could think that she had been there in Winterfell when Tyrion Lannister and Jon Snow, two outcasts of society, met in the castle courtyard in the very first episode, and she had taken little Tyrion's statement ("Never forget what you are. The rest of the world will not. Wear it like armor and it can never be used to hurt you.", Episode 1.01 *Winter is Coming*) literally and made it her own.

I found, and still find, this "perfect imperfection", the combination of an outwardly strong but also internally vulnerable character, who is forced into the role of an outsider because she deviates from the social norm and who must always work hard to earn acceptance (I shall not even mention respect) due to a lack of feminine charisma, truly fascinating. And this ultimately contributed to the fact that Brienne became my favorite character over the course of the story.

Over to you, Ms. Christie!

Nevertheless, the all-important criterion is undoubtedly the actress herself. Above all, a film character is brought to life by the way that they are embodied by their respective actor (or actress in this case). And I honestly cannot say for certain whether I would have been so enthusiastic about Brienne if she had been played by anyone other than Gwendoline Tracey Philippa Christie (her full name). A woman who is as extraordinary and likable as her series character.

Along with Brienne's first appearance in the third episode of the second season, *What is Dead May Never Die*, Christie's name also appears in the end credits of that episode for the first time.

14

Her name remains in the end credits until the end of season three. This changes at the beginning of season four when her name can be seen in the opening credits of *Two Swords*, due to her more significant storyline and the associated leap into the extended main cast.

Brienne had become a real fan favorite over the course of the seasons, especially in Great Britain and the United States, and her roller coaster odyssey with Jaime Lannister, beginning at the end of the second season and extending over the entire third season, ranks among the most popular storylines of all time in fan circles.

Even Gwendoline Christie herself is surprised at "how much people have taken this character to their hearts" (source: scoopnest.com).

The fact that the now 38-year-old British stage actress is able to portray this complex character so convincingly is certainly also because the role of Brienne is essentially tailor-made for Christie. Even the actress herself was often teased because of her height during her childhood. However, she no longer wishes to talk about that; she suffered too much back then.

It therefore seems like an ironic twist of fate that Christie, who was born in the English south coast town of Worthing/Sussex and has now been living in London for some time, now owes her sudden and unexpected success as an actress and thus partly her growing popularity to this apparent burden.

In retrospect, her life would have taken a completely different course if a spinal cord injury suffered at the age of twelve due to a growth spurt, and thus a tragic circumstance for her, had not brought her to acting in the first place and forced her to give up her actual career choice. She originally wanted to be a ballet dancer.

It was the combination of expression and discipline that she loved so much about this sport. She eventually decided on a career as an actress and applied to the Drama Centre in London a few years later.

Despite graduating with honors from there in 2005, she was kindly told that she would find it difficult to get suitable role offers in the future due to her size. From then on, she earned her living primarily by performing in Shakespeare plays. In 2007, Christie celebrated her screen debut with the British sci-fi short film *The Time Surgeon* known only to real insiders. A small role in Terry Gilliam's *The Imaginarium of Doctor Parnassus* two years later in 2009 was her career highlight at that time, until her big moment finally came in 2011:

"When life gives you lemons, make lemonade."

A motto that could hardly have been more appropriate when she learned that her name was increasingly being mentioned on the internet in connection with a yet-to-be-cast role in *Game of Thrones*. And she fulfilled the decisive criteria for the role with her size and acting training. She started reading Martin's books, which she had never heard of before, and she watched the first season of the series. From then on, she did not give up. This was her opportunity to portray "Brienne of Tarth", a woman who does not correspond to the classic image of women and does not define herself by her femininity; it was her role, and she had to get it. At all costs.

In this respect, she gave the following answer in an interview with "Elle Magazine" some time ago:

"This is the part I always wanted to play but never knew existed. All the things I had wanted to cloak about myself, that I felt a little ashamed and embarrassed about, had been bullied for, these things had a place they could live – in Brienne."

In order to meet the visual and physical requirements demanded of her by the role, Christie had to make some sacrifices. First of all, she had to lose her long hair. A change of her personality which not only took a lot of effort but which also brought out a lot of tears, as she later admitted. This was followed by several weeks of yoga, horse riding, sword fighting and stage fighting training. She eventually lost several kilograms of weight and gained muscle mass through a change of diet. She pretty much pulled out all the stops to get this role. This is despite the fact that, before becoming involved in *Game of Thrones*, she was actually "someone who liked to lie on the couch and eat chocolates." (source: melty.de).

Christie, who was not only invited to the casting for the role of "Brienne" but also to have it given to her, ultimately proved to be a very fortunate choice, not just for the two key *Game of Thrones* producers David Benioff and D.B. Weiss.

Michael Slovis, the director of the first two episodes of season five of the series (*The Wars to Come* and *The House of Black and White*), also raved about collaborating with Christie and her co-star Daniel Portman, who plays her companion "Podrick Payne":

"They are the nicest, sweetest, most fun-loving, talented, open, creative... I could go on for half an hour with this, and they are just the most wonderful people to work with. Look at Gwendoline. I could sit and watch her read the New York City phone book for three hours and I wouldn't be bored. She's so beautiful and so committed and so in the moment of being that character." (source: esquire.com)

What's more, this view is shared by Kristofer Hivju who plays the Wildling leader Tormund Giantsbane. Some time ago, the Norwegian told the "Hollywood Reporter" that filming the scenes with Gwendoline Christie for the fourth and fifth episodes of season six (*Book of the Stranger* and *The Door*) was a very special highlight for him:

"I love working with her. She's a fantastic actress. She's so much fun. She's filled with life. (...)."

First minor successes and mega blockbusters

Without any exaggeration, Christie definitely succeeded in making her acting breakthrough with "Brienne" and her name will probably always be linked to this character in the same way as Sean Connery is to "James Bond" or Daniel Radcliffe is to "Harry Potter". However, she was also active in film and television aside from this global phenomenon, even if only in rather smaller productions that were not nearly as successful as the HBO hit *Game of Thrones*.

For example, she played "Lexi" as part of the main cast in the first two seasons (out of three) of the rather unknown British sci-fi TV series *Wizards vs. Aliens* (2012/13), which was co-produced by the BBC, and where the extra-terrestrial "Nekross" feast on the magic of all the wizards on earth. Don't worry, it is as bizarre as it sounds. The German television audience has been deprived of this show so far, perhaps because it was just too whacky.

Furthermore, in addition to the aforementioned *The Imaginarium of Doctor Parnassus*, she worked with director Terry Gilliam again. However, she only got a mini role in *The Zero Theorem* in 2013. And when I say "mini", I really mean mini, as her face can only be seen for a few seconds in a street commercial.

Speaking of 2013, she eventually came to the attention of the major Hollywood studios this year, and thus she then played parts in two globally successful blockbusters at the end of 2015: *The Hunger Games: Mockingjay, Part 2* and *Star Wars: Episode VII – The Force Awakens*. However, both projects were based on completely different and admittedly fortunate circumstances. While Christie owes her not particularly spectacular role as "Commander Lyme" in the fourth and final part of the *Hunger Games* trilogy to the originally cast actress, Lily Rabe, who dropped out because of scheduling difficulties, she was active and worked hard to promote herself for the *Star Wars* role. Once she learned that Disney Studios intended to shoot a new *Star Wars* film, she really wanted to be in it "like a dog with a bone" (source: faz.net). She was successful as we now know since she eventually got the role of chrome armor-wearing "Captain Phasma", though it was not the original plan to get to this point. Director J.J. Abrams, in consultation with his screenwriter Lawrence Kasdan, only decided to cast the originally male character of the Captain as a woman shortly before shooting.

As Captain Phasma, the commander of the "First Order's" force of stormtroopers, Christie is not only the first female antagonist in the *Star Wars* universe but she also proves that, in addition to playing the virtuous "Brienne", she can also feel at home on the

"Dark Side of the Force". **SPOILER ALERT!** Unfortunately for her, her (sadly fairly modest) screen presence ends in a trash compactor and the Starkiller Base of the First Order is also destroyed shortly thereafter. However, her return as "Phasma" in the forthcoming *Episode VIII - The Last Jedi* (cinema release: December 2017) is already certain. Supposedly, there should be much more to see of the "Captain" than was the case in Episode Seven. I think this is excellent news.

Perhaps we will then be able to see her face at some point that did not happen in *The Force Awakens*. But whether she is wearing a helmet or not, her silver and chrome armor probably already has cult status.

Unfortunately, last year in 2016, Gwendoline Christie only appeared once on the big screen at the start of September in *Absolutely Fabulous: The Movie*, the film adaptation of the eponymous 1990s British cult comedy series. She plays herself in several short cameo appearances.

This film had an unbelievably star-studded cast and it was just as unrestrained, sharp and overtly socially critical as could be expected from this format.

Absolutely loopy!

A remarkable development

Since the beginning of her film career in *The Time Surgeon*, it is particularly striking that Gwendoline Christie has been predominantly cast in productions in the sci-fi or fantasy genre. I do not believe that this is pure coincidence. Special films sometimes simply require extraordinary actors who stand out from the crowd.

And so she does, just because of her size alone. In this respect, her involvement in the second season of the TV crime series *Top of the Lake*, which should find its way to our television screens later this year, offers a successful counter project. I am already fascinated by the idea of seeing her in a modern police uniform for a change, rather than medieval or futuristic armor. However, the name of her role had not been defined by the time this book was published.

In fact, after the first season, which I found rather slow and sometimes lacking tension, I had no intention of watching a second season if there was one. However, I have changed my mind in the meantime. It is quite interesting how Ms. Christie can achieve all this...

It was undoubtedly very unfortunate and a crucial episode in her life to have to give up the sport she loved but every now and then one door closes and another, significantly greater door opens. And I hope, no, I am sure, that we will see much more of her in the future.

But it is not only in her various film roles where she cuts a fine figure. Even when she is off camera at so-called panels or public appearances such as film premieres, she is a very welcome guest due to her cheerful nature and her almost infectious blithesomeness which she spreads everywhere in sharp contrast to the rather grumpy "Brienne".

Alison "Boom" Baumgartner put this very eloquently in her article on sciencefiction.com where she described an interview from March 2015 with Christie at the Denver ComicCon as "a delight" and then gave a piece of advice for all *Game of Thrones* fans:

"(...) so for all of you *Game of Thrones* fans, if you have a chance to catch one of her panels at another con, be sure to get in line early! It will be worth it!"

The organizers of the *Star Wars* Celebration in London in mid-July last year went one step further when they showed great trust in inviting Christie not as a guest but as the moderator of the panel discussion on the new *Star Wars* spin-off *Rogue One: A Star Wars Story*.

A trust that Christie more than repaid according to one Twitter user ("Having @lovegwendoline [Gwendoline Christie's Twitter Account] host the *Rogue One* panel was one of the best planning decisions in @SW_Celebration (...).").

As if she had never done anything else before, she commemorated the 80 victims of the recent attack in Nice/France in a moving speech at the beginning of the panel and let her tears flow freely when the audience spontaneously began singing "La Marseillaise".
A truly magnificent and emotional appearance!

Unfortunately, I have not yet been able to see Gwendoline Christie live anywhere. When you do not live in the United Kingdom or the USA, the chances of seeing her in person are limited since most of these conventions or film premieres take place there.
But I will never lose hope...

A brief outlook on Season Seven
First let us move casually to the seventh and thus penultimate season of *Game of Thrones*, as confirmed by HBO which has sadly been reduced to seven episodes.
Even though many fans of the series (myself included) find it hard to imagine that filming will soon be wrapped, whether we like it or not, we must come to terms with the fact that even a ground-breaking format such as *GoT* is finite after all.
Like probably every fan of the series, I am of course eager to find out what happens this year. And it should now come as no surprise that I am particularly itching to learn what is next for Brienne and Podrick. The last thing we saw of the two was their escape by boat from Riverrun which is now occupied by the Lannisters and Freys.

I know that you should not have a favorite in a format such as *Game of Thrones* since it is well known that this series does not hold back when it comes to unexpectedly snatching our favorites away from us. Eddard Stark's honesty, a virtue that would probably have been the decisive reason to allow the character to live until the end of any other series, ultimately became his fatal downfall. This negative example alone is reason enough to suspect that Brienne undoubtedly belongs to the group of people who run the serious risk of being killed off in every episode. She is ultimately one of the few remaining honorable characters who puts the welfare of other people above her own without seeking glory or financial reward, who raises the audiences' hope for a victory of good over evil, and who thus represents a silver lining on the horizon of the rather gloomy *Game of Thrones* universe. And this awareness ultimately leads to my dilemma: on the one hand, I look forward to every minute of her screen presence but on the other, I am aware that every scene could lead to her death. To be honest, I cannot imagine that the series creators would let a character like Brienne simply die off screen in passing. Yet, should the time come and if she does not live until the end of the story, then I hope that she dies for a greater cause, for good, and that she sacrifices herself so that someone else can live. That would be in her spirit, truly knightly and, above all, the farewell Brienne deserves. But fortunately, this is just pure speculation and it would be a pity, in my opinion, if this was to happen. In that case, I would then have to seriously consider who to cheer on in the last remaining episodes. Or, to put it in the (slightly modified) words of German humorist Loriot who died in 2011:

**"Game of Thrones" without "Brienne" is possible,
but pointless.**

What happened previously...

A look back at the events in episodes 1.01 – 2.02

After King Robert Baratheon's early and unexpected death, an unrelenting dispute over his successor broke out between several contenders, also known as the "War of the Five Kings".

This conflict was triggered by the fact that Eddard Stark, former Lord of Winterfell and "Hand of the King" during Robert's lifetime, discovered that Robert's eldest son and designated successor, Joffrey, was not Robert's natural son but rather the result of an incestuous relationship between his mother, Queen Cersei Baratheon, and her twin brother, Jaime Lannister. Thus, Eddard denied Joffrey any rightful claim to the Iron Throne.

When he threatened to reveal this secret and henceforth supported Robert's younger brother Stannis' claim to the throne, he was betrayed by Petyr Baelish, a member of the "Small Council", and Janos Slynt, Commander of the City Watch in King's Landing, and ultimately beheaded for high treason at the behest of King Joffrey.

Eddard's eldest son Robb took up arms and mobilized all vassals of House Stark, initially to free his father from the dungeons of the Red Keep, but then later to take revenge for his death.

Even though his father Eddard considered Robert's younger brother Stannis' claim to be rightful, Robb decided to seek an alliance with Renly Baratheon, the youngest of the three Baratheon brothers, as well as his ally, the rich House Tyrell.

After his eldest brother's death, Renly, in fear of his life, therefore fled the capital together with Loras Tyrell, the heir to Highgarden and also his brother-in-law, because despite having the weakest claim of all contenders to the Iron Throne, he also claimed it himself and thus bypassed Robert's supposed son Joffrey.

Even in comparison to his older brother Stannis, the Lord of Storm's End saw himself as the better suited king:

"This isn't about the bloody line of succession. (…) We all know what Stannis is. He inspires no love or loyalty. He is not a king. I am. (…) Do you still believe good soldiers make good kings?" - **Renly Baratheon to Eddard Stark (Episode 1.07 *You Win or You Die*)**

Robb, now proclaimed as the "King in the North" by his bannermen, subsequently sends his mother Catelyn to negotiations with Renly Baratheon to the South in the Stormlands to secure his support in the forthcoming war.

Season Two

Episode 2.03

What is Dead May Never Die

Location:
Renly Baratheon's camp at Bitterbridge, Stormlands

Having barely arrived at Renly's camp, Catelyn Stark watches the final battle of a knight's tournament in which the previously mentioned Ser Loras Tyrell faces an unknown knight.

Only their conspicuous bronze armor and shield – yellow sun on a rose colored field and white crescents on a blue field, quartered – provide information about their origin.

It comes as a surprise to the surrounding crowd when the unknown knight finally manages to defeat their opponent who has already won numerous tournaments and who is in a secret (at least he hopes so) same-sex relationship with Renly.

The victor ultimately complies with Renly's request to approach and remove their helmet, and the crowd including Ser Loras is more than surprised that it is not the face of a man that emerges as expected, but rather that of a woman – that of **Brienne of Tarth**.

Since I had not yet read Martin's series *A Song of Ice and Fire* at that time (something that I have now corrected), I must admit that in that moment I was also extremely surprised by who was under the helmet. I was pleasantly surprised, to tell the truth. Even if, at that time, the character of "Brienne" did not fascinate me in the same way as she would later and I was not yet compelled to write a book about her, I found her to be very likable and an enhancement to the story from the beginning. I even admit that I found it kind of "cool" that the slightly narcissistic Loras Tyrell, who was used to winning, was defeated by a woman of all people.

Yet, as unexpected as Brienne's victory is, one person is hardly surprised by the outcome and has no doubt in her ability to be victorious in such a tournament: Renly Baratheon.
He grants Brienne a wish that he would fulfil if it were in his power.

"Your Grace, I ask the honor of a place in your Kingsguard. I will be one of your seven, pledge my life to yours and keep you safe from all harm." **- Brienne to Renly Baratheon**

When she respectfully kneels before Renly to ask him for a place in his Kingsguard, her choice of forceful words impressively demonstrates how very different she is from other female characters and provides the viewer with a wonderful first insight into her mindset influenced by knightly virtues.

With Renly's call to rise as "Brienne of the Kingsguard", a look at her proud face reveals that her lifelong dream is ultimately fulfilled.

The Lord of Storm's End is now finally ready to hear Catelyn Stark's reason for her appearance so far south. But he abruptly ends their conversation a short time later when he is disgruntled by her comment that he would perhaps not take the war seriously enough and asks Brienne to escort his guest to her tent.

"I fought for my king. Soon I'll fight for him on the battlefield. Die for him if I must. And, if it please you, Brienne's enough. I'm no lady." - **Brienne to Catelyn Stark**

At this juncture, when Catelyn Stark praises Brienne for her courage in the tournament and addresses her as "Lady Brienne" befitting her status without knowing that she is on thin ice, the Maiden of Tarth reveals another example of her philosophy of life. She impressively emphasizes that, despite her noble origin as the daughter of a Lord, she not only places no value on her social status but she would prefer to lose it entirely.

The resonant pride in Brienne's voice is unmistakable; she has finally achieved what she had sought her whole life and she considers Renly to be "her" true King, despite knowing that his claim to the title is the weakest of all the contenders.

D uring a subsequent intimate encounter in Renly's tent, Loras Tyrell shows that he is still frustrated by his painful defeat to Brienne in the tournament.

It is quite clear that his welts and bruises are not nearly as painful as the fact that he lost to a woman. To make matters worse, Renly then fulfilled this woman's wish by appointing her to his Kingsguard which is downright humiliating for the "Knight of the Flowers"

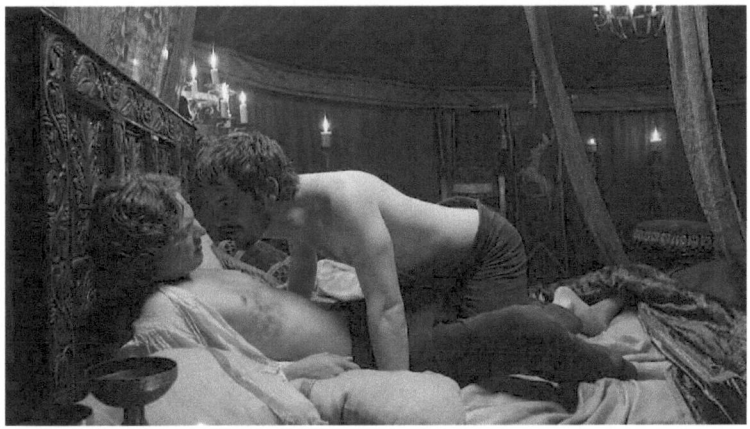

The fact that Loras patronizingly calls his defeater "Brienne the Beauty" in this context underlines his frustration fairly clearly. However, I do not think that this is meant personally since, apart from defeating him in the tournament, she had not previously given him any reason to hold a grudge against her.

In my opinion, he only uses this statement as an outlet to express his disappointment. Generally speaking, since he is looking for a supposed weakness of the person concerned so that he can look at himself in the mirror again,

Brienne's external appearance provides a wonderful target...

By contrast, Renly's description of Brienne as a "very capable warrior", who adores him, reveals that he very much appreciates those skills that ultimately knocked Loras into the dust and that he can be absolutely sure of her loyalty to him.

These words cannot significantly alleviate Loras' disappointment, though.

Garden of Bones

Location:
Renly Baratheon's camp at Storm's End, Stormlands

A s a new member of Renly's Kingsguard, Brienne has the honor of being present for his conversation with Petyr Baelish, named "Littlefinger", who has travelled to the Stormlands for negotiations. Brienne's presence suggests that there is a very special relationship between the Lord of Storm's End and the woman.

Littlefinger, who owes his nickname to his small body size in childhood and his origin from the Fingers, a coastal region in the Vale of Arryn, played a significant role in the deceit and ultimate execution of Eddard Stark, the former Hand of the King and Lady Catelyn's husband.

Nevertheless, Renly agrees to listen to the concerns of the member of the Small Council and active brothel operator but he makes it clear that he does not want their conversation to go on any longer than necessary.

The exciting thing here is Renly's sharp-tongued reaction to Littlefinger's wink suggesting that it would be better to have the conversation in private, when he tells Baelish that Brienne's loyalty comes without charge and that she can be trusted completely. This is certainly no coincidence since Littlefinger's so-called loyalty is usually with those from who he hopes to gain either financial or social advantages. Or both.

Ultimately, Renly not only hears fear for his position in the royal court in Baelish's remarks but also fear for his own life. Should the Lord of Storm's End actually manage to conquer the Iron Throne with the help of his giant army, Littlefinger, a traitor to Renly and also in the service of the Lannisters, would be a defeated enemy and thus in acute danger of losing his life.

To avoid standing on the potential loser's side in the end, Littlefinger contemplates a change of sides and offers Renly "open gates" to King's Landing instead of a protracted siege.

Even though Brienne, who is incidentally wearing the Kingsguard cloak for the first time, is only a silent observer in the scene, she immediately gets a wonderful impression of Petyr Baelish and his opportunistic turncoat mentality and sycophantic manner.

| Location: |
| **Coast near Storm's End, Stormlands** |

Accompanied by their respective Kingsguards and their closest confidants, including Brienne on Renly's side, the two Baratheon brothers Renly and Stannis, who are both fighting for the Iron Throne, meet on the coast of the Stormlands.

Both opponents have not seen each other for a long time, and Stannis is surprised to see Catelyn Stark on his brother's side, even though her late husband Eddard supported his claim to the Iron Throne, ultimately costing him his life.

Despite their common enemy in the form of Joffrey Baratheon and the Lannisters, Stannis is unwilling to form an alliance with his younger brother. He stands by his view that he has the right to the throne and that anyone who denies this is his enemy.

Since Renly makes no effort to bow to his older brother, though, Stannis gives him a choice: surrender before the next dawn or be destroyed.
With confidence in the numerical superiority of his armies, Renly does not respond to this threat and both parties finally go their separate ways without having come any closer.

As before in the conversation between Renly and Petyr Baelish, Brienne is just a listener and does not actively contribute to the parley. Nevertheless, this discussion between the two pretenders to the throne is enormously important for her.

On the one hand, she now learns the extent to which the rivalry for the Iron Throne has turned the brothers into fierce enemies through Renly's verbal barbs and Stannis' supercool and unyielding manner and that neither of the two are willing to give in on this point.

On the other hand, she encounters Melisandre, a priestess of the red god R'hllor, in Stannis' entourage, and thus a woman, whose message to Renly ("Look to your sins, Lord Renly. The night is dark and full of terrors.") truly does not bode well at the end of the dispute...

The Ghost of Harrenhal

Location:
Renly Baratheon's camp at Storm's End, Stormlands

With her new role as Renly's personal bodyguard, Brienne is also present on the evening before the imminent battle, when the youngest of the three Baratheon brothers and Catelyn Stark negotiate the conditions of a mutual alliance in his tent.

Since Catelyn's son Robb is only going to war with the Lannisters out of revenge for the execution of his father and he has no interest in the Iron Throne according to his mother, Renly agrees that her son may continue to call himself King in the North. The only condition is that her son Robb swears an oath of fealty to him.

When black smoke suddenly rushes into the tent, takes a human-like form and then, without warning, stabs the pretender to the throne through the back during mid-conversation and ultimately kills him before the eyes of a stunned

Brienne, this undoubtedly represents one of the key scenes for her further storyline.

This murder shatters her recently fulfilled dream in one swift blow, and it is now known what Melisandre's threatening words were all about. However, we do not yet know why this event shocked the woman so profoundly.

Of course, it is particularly tragic for Brienne that the ominous shadow vanishes into thin air at that moment. Thus, there is no conceivable perpetrator – except her herself.

Alerted by the noise inside the tent, two Kingsguards storm into it and see Brienne bent over Renly's lifeless body. There is no alternative, the two Kingsguards regard her as the perpetrator and immediately attack the surprised and horrified woman.

Even though she is close to despair, she is able to kill both opponents in the end.

For the first time, all of Brienne's sword skills are put to the test, and she really is in a class of her own. The brutality and ruthlessness she uses to overcome the two enemies to defend herself are truly impressive.

The fact that she then does not want to leave the victim's side proves that the Maiden of Tarth is absolutely not a rationally acting person, as described above. As Catelyn bluntly makes her aware, despite the imminent danger, it is martyr-like to be hanged for wanting to remain by the side of a dead man out of pure loyalty (or perhaps even out of love?). Of course, Brienne is not to blame for Renly's murder.

However, the lynch mob would not care about that.

Only thanks to her unequivocal words ("You can't avenge him if you're dead!") and simultaneous appeal for vengeance directed at Brienne can Catelyn Stark eventually motivate the devastated and disillusioned woman to flee Renly's camp together with her...

Location:
Renly Baratheon's camp at Storm's End, Stormlands

---

hile Loras Tyrell and his sister Margaery mourn the laid-out body of his brother-in-law or her husband in his tent, Loras' sister suggests that Brienne killed

Renly. She presumably drew her (non-expressed) conclusions from the facts that she would have been the only person at least theoretically capable of doing it and she also fled afterwards.

Yet, her brother Loras immediately contradicts her, and since Margaery has no response, one can assume that she does not really believe that the woman had anything to do with Renly's murder. She admired him too much for that. Brienne did not have the slightest reason to kill him.

Loras, Margaery and Petyr Baelish, who eventually also entered the tent, agree that there is only one person who will primarily profit from Renly's death shortly before the imminent battle – his older brother Stannis...

Location:
Kingswood, Stormlands

During a rest break on their escape from possible pursuers, it becomes clear that the two women have made completely different observations on who, or rather: what murdered Renly.

While it was only a shadow in the shape of a man for Cate-lyn Stark, Brienne has a completely different opinion. The tall woman is absolutely sure that the shadow took the form of Stannis Baratheon, Renly's older brother.

The extent to which Brienne is guided by her code of honor becomes clear when, although she does not express it, Catelyn feels that her companion wants to avenge the murder of Renly. Terms such as honor and loyalty are still of importance to Brienne far beyond death and she wastes absolutely no time thinking that her plan could be doomed to failure from the outset due to the numerical superiority of the opposing side.

Only when Catelyn Stark strongly persuades her that her possible death would serve absolutely no one and that Stan-nis is also an enemy of her son Robb, Brienne finally gives in and surprisingly offers her services to her counterpart instead of her eldest son.

"I do not know your son, my lady. But I could serve you, if you would have me." - **Brienne to Catelyn Stark**

As a result of Renly's sudden death and the associated dissolution of his Kingsguard, Brienne lost what she had sought her whole life: to be in the service of a gracious Lord, to serve him and to protect him by giving her life if necessary. Although the blonde woman and the northerner get to know each other a little better during their escape and Brienne cannot know whether Lady Stark really is who she claims to be, the tall woman admires and respects her courage to help their escape with a cool head, as well as her unwavering love for her children which becomes apparent during their conversation. These insights clearly seem more than sufficient for her to regard Lady Stark as worthy of her loyalty and service.

"Then I am yours, my lady. I will shield your back and give my life for yours, if it comes to that. I swear it by the Old Gods and the New." - **Brienne to Catelyn Stark**

Brienne only insists that she promises that she will not prevent her from taking revenge on Stannis when the time comes. Agreeing to this condition, Catelyn Stark accepts Brienne into her service.

The moment when Brienne solemnly places her sword between herself and Catelyn, kneels before her and swears her allegiance to her without making too much fuss about it is still one of my favorite scenes across storyline.

In my opinion, the background music of Ramin Djawadi's "The Old Gods and the New" gives this already moving scene an even more emotional touch. Incidentally, it is a piece with high recognition value because we shall hear it more often in very similar scenes...

Episode 2.06
The Old Gods and the New

The two women finally reach the camp of Catelyn's son Robb without further incident. The King in the North is equally surprised and pleased to see his mother again so soon and he presents Talisa Maegyr, a foreigner from Volantis, who is helping him care for the wounded.

Catelyn quickly realizes that her son and the attractive foreign woman are clearly connected by more than just work, and she reminds him that he is already promised to another woman ("You have inherited your father's responsibilities. I'm afraid they come at a cost. (...) You are promised to another. A debt that must be paid.").

In return for allowing Robb and his troops to cross the Green Fork of the Trident over the "Twins", the seat of House Frey, on his campaign to the South at that time,

Walder Frey demanded that Robb marry one of his numerous (and admittedly not very attractive) daughters or granddaughters, among other things.

Now in the service of Catelyn Stark, Brienne respectfully remains in the background during Catelyn's brief discussion with her son Robb.
It would have certainly been interesting to hear her opinion on Robb's plans to marry a woman other than the woman he is sworn to, and thus break an oath. A person who, like her, holds moral values so dogmatically, could not actually approve of this out of principle.

A Man without Honor

Location:
Robb Stark's camp at Oxcross, Westerlands

Jaime Lannister, named "Kingslayer", because he stabbed his King Aerys II. in the back during the Sack of King's Landing, even though he had sworn to protect him, was captured by Robb Stark's troops during the Battle of the Whispering Wood.

After many months imprisoned in a muddy cage, he eventually managed to escape, during which he first murdered his fellow prisoner, his cousin Alton Lannister, and then Torrhen Karstark, a son of Stark vassal Lord Rickard Karstark, who was guarding him.

Nevertheless, this escape is short-lived since the Kingslayer is quickly caught and brought back the camp.

The way in which Brienne abruptly stops the Stark man from entering the tent, who wants to give Catelyn Stark the message from the recaptured prisoner Jaime Lannister ("Don't enter without an invitation, man!"), beautifully illustrates her previously described problems with men rooted in her past.

As Catelyn immediately makes her way to the prisoner together with Brienne, Jaime Lannister finds himself surrounded by angered Stark and Karstark men, especially Rickard Karstark, the Lord of Karhold, who would prefer to execute him on the spot for murdering his son.

With great difficulty and the clear message that Jaime Lannister is the prisoner of his Lord Robb Stark and not an object to satisfy his personal desire for vengeance, Catelyn manages to prevent the temperamental father from taking instant revenge for the murder of his son in the absence of her son Robb.

Lord Karstark is furious to be deprived of his vengeance and he eventually leaves Catelyn standing at the end of a fierce dispute. But he seems to be far from finished with the murderer of his son.

In this scene Brienne already has the opportunity to show that her oath of allegiance was not just empty words: by energetically shouting "Treason!" and simultaneously, instinctively intimating that she will draw her sword, she makes it clear to Lord Karstark what she thinks of his disrespectful and unfounded accusation of her Lady whose son Robb had left the camp to have fun with his beloved, not for negotiations.

As a side issue, Brienne gains a brief but absolutely characteristic impression of Jaime Lannister's arrogance and complacency for the first time here. Even though he is certainly not in a position to be arrogant at this time, he does not pass up the opportunity to turn on his dubious charm while kneeling in the mud. Irritated by his sarcastic remarks, Catelyn eventually has him locked up.

Location:
Robb Stark's camp at Oxcross, Westerlands

On the following evening, Catelyn Stark and Brienne observe from afar how obviously drunk Stark and Karstark men are disputing over what to do with the Kingslayer. The majority of Karstarks are loudly calling for his head.

"The Kingslayer won't last the night. The more they drink, the angrier they'll get. And when the Karstarks draw their swords... Who wants to die defending a Lannister?"
- **Brienne to Catelyn Stark**

Brienne's presumption that he will probably not survive the night and the following addition that no one would be willing to sacrifice their life for the Kingslayer, which is rather untypical for her and with a cynical undertone, prompts Lady Catelyn to act. With a concise "Come!", she calls on Brienne to follow her.

The two women enter the Kingslayer's pen, and despite Catelyn making him aware of the tangible danger that he would probably not see the following day due to Torrhen Karstark's murder, he subsequently provokes Lady Stark with his sarcastic views of chivalry ("Any knight would have done the same.") and questions the entire philosophy of vows since one would eventually be forced to break one of his vows. At the latest when one's loyalty to a third party turns against one's own family.

The arrogance of the Kingslayer, which was already shown in the previous scene, is also noticeable here. He positively enjoys showcasing his verbal dominance over the two women and persistently compromising them.
Even our protagonist, who remains in the background and thus completely out of the conversation, becomes the target of his biting taunts to Catelyn Stark ("Is that a woman? (…) Where did you find this beast?"). Even though these insults are not new to Brienne, Catelyn instantly takes her out of the firing line, where not only does she describe Brienne as

a "true knight" in comparison to the prisoner but she denies him this dignity as a "man without honor".

Of course, this is an accusation that Jaime Lannister does not stand for. He immediately, sarcastically confronts Lady Stark with the extramarital indiscretion of her late husband and Jon Snow, the resulting bastard whom she hated from day one ("(...) The walking, talking reminder that the honorable Lord Eddard Stark has fucked another woman."). A statement with which he not only drags his honor through the mud posthumously but also adds more salt to Catelyn's wound. It is hardly surprising that these words make her face flush with anger.

Due to the deliberate scene end, the viewer can only assume what Catelyn actually intends to do with Brienne's sword when she asks for it in this moment...

The Prince of Winterfell

Location:
north of Hornvale, in the Woods near the Red Fork of the Trident, Riverlands

When Petyr "Littlefinger" Baelish was involved in negotiations in Renly Baratheon's camp, he searched for Catelyn Stark, who was also present at the time, at the behest of Tyrion Lannister, Jaime's little brother and acting Hand of the King in the absence of his father Tywin at that time. His words clearly had an effect on her when he showed her an opportunity to see her two daughters Arya and Sansa again who were supposedly still in the capital and thus hostages of the Lannisters:

"The Lannisters will trade your daughters for the Kingslayer." - **Petyr Baelish to Catelyn Stark (Episode 2.04** *Garden of Bones***)**

However, and this is where Littlefinger's cunning behavior comes into play, on the one hand, only Sansa is in the capital, while Arya was able to escape immediately after the beheading of her father Eddard and, on the other hand, the Lannister's desire to make this trade was Tyrion Lannister's idea alone. Cersei, Tyrion's and Jaime's sister, only commissioned Baelish to find Arya.
But, as suspected by Tyrion, Littlefinger obviously hit a nerve with Catelyn, and he was able to appeal to her maternal instinct when he added that her children were seemingly safe but no one knew for how long...

"(...) But you know the Queen and you know Joffrey. I fear for the longevity if they remain in the capital. (...) Consider it, Cat. You may not get another chance."
- **Petyr Baelish to Catelyn Stark (Episode 2.04** *Garden of Bones***)**

Even though Catelyn knows that she is giving away her son Robb's trump card and thus weakening his position, she eventually gives Brienne the order to take the Kingslayer to the capital to trade him for her two daughters. They leave under the cover of night...

atelyn's reaction to Brienne's comment that the Kingslayer would probably not survive the night, now makes sense. She had to prevent this from happening. A dead Jaime consequently means no trade, and no trade means no daughters.

We also now learn why Lady Stark asked for Brienne's sword. At the end of the previous episode, we had to assume that she was about to do something really bad but it ultimately only served the purpose of freeing the Kingslayer and putting her plan into action.

Ironically, this tight-lipped woman now has her mission with Jaime Lannister, one of the biggest and inflated attention seekers in Westeros, at her throat.

Upon arriving at the Red Fork of the Trident, Brienne decides to continue the difficult path ahead towards the river on foot and lets the two horses go free.

When she pulls the Kingslayer off his horse in a not exactly gentle manner and removes the bag from his head intended to make orientation difficult for him, she must immediately endure the first verbal lashing; he once again takes aim at her appearance ("You're much uglier in daylight.").

However, this comment still bounces off her. Still.

Jaime continuously tries to strike up a conversation with Brienne on the path to the riverbank. But, apart from revealing her name, the woman sees no reason to talk to her hostage. She is only focused on her mission to bring him to the capital as intact as possible.

Jaime senses that Brienne has a very obvious dislike for him, and he has fun asserting his verbal dominance and incessantly compromising her with his cynical and offensive remarks. However, when her hostage's comments eventually move towards perverse sexual preferences ("Have you known many men? (…) Women? Horses?") and her appearance yet again, she must force herself not to attack a handcuffed man.

When, shortly thereafter, she sees a bridge over the river and immediately roughly pushes her prisoner to the ground to seek cover behind a bush, this very nicely reveals Brienne's aforementioned contempt of all those who have broken their knightly oath.

"All my life men like you have sneered at me. And all my life I've been knocking men like you into the dust!"
- **Brienne to Jaime Lannister**

She snappily responds ("Your crimes are past forgiveness, Kingslayer. (…) You've harmed others, those you were sworn to protect, the weak, the innocent!") to Jaime's rather half-hearted apology when he mockingly asks what he has done to her.

But, even Brienne's abrupt but true words do not stop him from wanting to throw her off balance with his idle talk, meanwhile she discovers a small rowboat on the riverbank and enters the water shortly thereafter.

With extreme discipline and pursuing her mission alone, Brienne does not enter any long verbal exchanges with the Kingslayer since, aside from her already existing dislike for him, she is very well aware of the fact that she is not equal to him verbally. Even when he questions her skills as a warrior and challenges her to a fair duel, she remains true to form (which is probably for the best, because with everything we have learned about the Kingslayer so far, who knows what he really means by "fair"?) and merely gives him the understanding that it could be a big mistake to underestimate her.

She eventually gets on the boat with him and continues her journey over water.

Perhaps some noticed the small rhetorical subtlety near the end of the scene: when Jaime senses that Brienne is not falling for his tricks and quips and then tries to provoke her by stating that there are only three men in Westeros who might have a chance against him in a duel, and that she is not one of them, his assessment is absolutely correct because Brienne is not a man...

Valar morghulis

Brienne and Jaime have now left the river and are making their way through the woods of the Riverlands on foot.

While the Kingslayer is still incessantly trying to verbally attack the woman, she notices three female corpses hanging from a broad branch above a forest clearing.

Jaime assumes that the three were tavern girls who served the soldiers of his father Tywin and were killed by Stark men for this reason.

However, before Brienne is able to cut the corpses down to bury them with dignity, they are both caught off guard by three Stark soldiers, and she must tell more than just one white lie to the three Northmen so as not to attract attention.

She must ultimately assume that pursuers tasked with re-capturing the Kingslayer are already on their heels.

Of course, Brienne is used to any form of ridicule. How-ever, when she merely tells the three probing Stark men that she is moving a prisoner and getting a roar of laughter because she is "a woman" and they would clearly not trust this task to her, her irritated facial expression alone shows how these insults are putting a strain on her again and again.

When the spokesman for the three Northmen later down-right gloats about being responsible for the murder of the three women with his two companions and that two of them were given quick deaths, but the third experienced a slow one, there is the realization that the girls had obviously fallen victim to their pure lust for murder, which does not go down well with the woman with the strong sense of jus-tice. Nevertheless, she does not let it show or provoke any response.

But, all of Brienne's attempts to deceive and get her ward and herself out of this predicament fail when one of the men finally recognizes Jaime as the Kingslayer after a long discussion.

Since her cover is almost blown, the woman has no other choice than to rush forward. Out of the blue and with cour-age born of desperation, she attacks and ultimately kills the perplexed men thanks to her tactical innovation in the end.

In this respect, her main advantage is certainly the fact that she is underestimated everywhere. Of course, this brings enormous potential for surprising her opponents, even if there are no ribbons or greeting cards... The ruth-lessness with which she works can be seen through the ex-ample of the spokesman who she saves for last. Filled with hatred and in terms of "quid pro quo", she pushes her sword into the lower abdomen of the man lying helplessly on the ground and makes him die a slow and painful death like one of the three tavern girls. Justice à la Brienne...

It is certainly not the case that Brienne sought this confrontation. Not even when the leader made her aware of the abuse and painful deaths of the three women. No, she wants to avoid the entire situation by making several excuses so that she is not noticed. Only when the three Stark men do not let up and she feels forced into a corner, she sees no alternative than to deal with the matter in her own way.

In the end, following the two Baratheon Kingsguards in *The Ghost of Harrenhal* (Episode 2.05), corpses three, four and five line her path to the South.
In my opinion, though, she did not have a genuine alternative in either situation.

Oh yes... What does the good Jaime actually do? While he was initially interested in continuously provoking her, he seemed visibly impressed by Brienne's merciless approach and she probably saved his life in the end.

However, rather than pointing out that she had actually killed her current allies by slaying the Stark men in a succinct and almost taunting manner at the end, a notion that she does not share at all ("I don't serve the Starks. I serve Lady Catelyn."), a simple "thank you" would have sufficed.

A Review of Season Two

That was it, Brienne's debut season.

When considering that this season primarily serves to introduce the character in the story and bring her closer to the viewer with all of her strengths and weaknesses, I think it is an outstanding success.
Brienne's introduction with her victory against Loras Tyrell in the knight's tournament was as extraordinary as the overall character is herself. Furthermore, we learn which life goals the Maiden of Tarth pursues and what is of primary importance to her relatively early on.

My favorite moments in this season were, firstly, the explosive demonstration of her swordsmanship and fighting skills in the fifth and tenth episode when she had to save her own skin twice, and, secondly, the oath of allegiance to Catelyn Stark in episode five. A truly great and touching scene where Brienne shows what she really is: a loyal and principled warrior who wants nothing more than to serve a good Lord or Lady.

If one were to give Brienne a report at the end, it would probably read: sword handling – excellent with honors, communication and social skills – comm... sorry, what?

However, having to endure the company of the Kingslayer and his incessant sarcasm for days on end is also an extremely unpleasant and thankless task. I do not believe that there is any one in the world who would actually enjoy it.

Season Three

Episode 3.02
Dark Wings, Dark Words

To avoid detection on their way to King's Landing, the unequal couple stay in the cover of the woods in the Riverlands.

However, rather than counting himself lucky for being protected by Brienne from very unpleasant potential consequences, Jaime starts off exactly where he finished before encountering the three Stark men, and tries to lure her with unpleasant topics of discussion from the reserves.

Not even a basic human need can stop him from poking around in his monosyllabic guard's past when he empties his bladder on a tree.

There is something quite entertaining about Brienne's desperate attempt to modestly look away while he relieves himself but it once more shows her awkwardness in non-everyday situations.

When he eventually harps on about the homosexuality of her adored Renly Baratheon and savagely belittles him ("(...) His proclivities were the worst kept secret at court. It's a shame the throne isn't made out of cocks. They'd have never got him off it."), he clearly touches a raw nerve for her.

He makes her so furious with this statement that she momentarily loses her temper. Filled with rage, she grabs him by the hair and warns him to shut his mouth with hatred in her eyes – a reaction that one would not have normally expected from such a usually extremely placid woman, unless one knows where to focus on her in this respect. Well, Jaime Lannister knew it.

Her prisoner knows that he probably went too far with his comments and he tries to smooth the waves again by not judging her or Renly for their feelings ("We don't get to choose who we love."). He does not exclude himself in this respect. After all, he has been in a relationship with his sister Cersei, which is not exactly socially acceptable, for many years. However, it is hard to believe that feelings of remorse or shame have now suddenly come over him. True to the motto "Once you've lost your reputation, you have nothing left to lose" he always dealt with it very directly after it came to light.

During the short subsequent encounter with a farmer, who happens to cross their path, Jaime realizes the possible risk that the man could have recognized him.

Brienne senses in the way the Kingslayer expresses this suspicion that he would rather see this unwelcome witness dead then and there to avoid exposure to the risk of being given away. Nevertheless, the woman does not see any reason for this. It simply goes against her knight's code to kill an innocent person who has not done anything to her or her ward, without reason and only on suspicion.
A stance that Jaime does not like at all.

His subsequent question, which is slightly reminiscent of Kaa, the snake from *The Jungle Book*, where he whispers in Brienne's ear as to whether the farmer is more innocent than the Stark daughters and whether his life is worth the risk of being given away and thus failing with the result that the girls would then also possibly be killed, clearly puts her in a moral conflict and makes her briefly question her moral values. Obviously overstrained by this dilemma, she simply pushes her hostage onwards without comment.

Location:
in the woods south of Mummer's Ford, at the Red Fork of the Trident, Riverlands

Brienne and Jaime reach another bridge over the Red Fork but crossing it would force them both out of cover

Despite the risk of being seen on the bridge and caught by possible pursuers, Jaime intentionally dawdles. With this trick, he is able to take advantage of a moment of her inattention to grab Brienne's second sword which she had previously taken off of one of the three dead Northmen. In this case, she was simply not smart enough to suspect that he had something up his sleeve.

If, until now, she has only faced ~~victims~~ ahem... I mean of course opponents who are not as talented as her, she now faces the following duel with one of the best swordsmen on the continent, even if he is possibly slightly out of practice due to his long period of captivity.

But while Jaime seriously intends to ditch his guard either way ("Bit of a quandary for you. If you kill me, you fail Lady Stark. But if you don't kill me, I'm going to kill you."), she indeed restrains herself as correctly judged by him. Brienne does not intend to hurt or kill her opponent and thus jeopardize her mission. Having to confess her failure (if at all possible) to Catelyn Stark would probably be her worst-case scenario!

However, it was all a waste of time in the end since Jaime's apparent cleverness in seizing a weapon to put his guard away unintentionally played into the hands of their pursuers. He certainly expected to be able to make short work of her, despite his chains and the fact that he had been imprisoned for a long time without training.

It takes a great deal of arrogance and ignorance to believe that he could simply rid himself of the woman in no time. It seems that he has already forgotten the lesson that Brienne gave the three Stark men. In any case, they both lose valuable time while dueling in the open field and ultimately being caught by their somehow expected chasers.

Based on their banner, the "Flayed Man", Jaime quickly realizes that the men are bannermen of House Bolton, vassals of House Stark. He acts clueless, though only until the moment where an old acquaintance of the two appears accompanying the Bolton men: the farmer who they previously encountered in the woods had recognized Jaime after all!

Locke, the leader of the Bolton men, eventually rewards the farmer with a bag of silver for his helpful tip and captures the hostage and his escort.

Of course, unlike Brienne, who was unwilling to waver from her chivalrous objective and her moral principles, Jaime's fear regarding the farmer was proven right, and his reproachful look towards her at the end is also quite understandable.

However, if he would have avoided this entirely unnecessary and stupid stunt from the outset, he would have been spared this great mess since he was already on the path to freedom and thus his sister...

..and we would have a completely different story from here on out.

Walk of Punishment

Location:
in the woods north of Tumbler's Fall, Riverlands

hile Brienne and Jaime are transported back to back on a horse as prisoners of the Bolton entourage and the men loudly sing "The Bear and the Maiden Fair" around them, the Kingslayer heavily blames the woman for their current situation, which is anything but pleasant. This, despite the fact that they were ultimately captured by their pursuers was largely due to his provocative manner and dawdling around. Self-reflection is obviously not one of his strengths...

"All my life I've been hearing: 'Jaime Lannister, what a brilliant swordsman.' You were slower than I expected. And more predictable. (...) Maybe you were as good as people said. Once. Or maybe people just love to overpraise a famous name." - **Brienne to Jaime Lannister**

Yet, unlike previous situations where she did not react to his verbal outpourings or reacted angrily, she now defends herself with counterarguments by questioning his preceding reputation as a swordsman, among other things.

Jaime appears to secretly agree with Brienne since he does not comment on her last verbal attack on his loss of class and skill.

Visibly affected by Brienne's comment, the Kingslayer then quickly changes the topic. He does not hold back when he tells his companion that she should expect something bad to happen to her later that day ("When we make camp tonight, you'll be raped. More than once. None of these fellows have ever been with a noblewoman. You'd be wise not to resist."), to then smugly add that she should simply pretend that "they're Renly".

Brienne suspects that Jaime may well be right with this threat but shows absolutely no comprehension of his view that, if he were in her position, he would rather be killed than let them have their way with him.

It is possible that this is just usual macho behavior being used to impress her. However, it is easy for a man to say such things.

In any case, Jaime achieved one thing with his comments – a rather concerned and thoughtful-looking Brienne...

Location:
in the woods north of Tumbler's Fall, Riverlands

As already indicated and anticipated by Jaime, Locke indeed intends to sexually assault the woman during the following night camp.

While Brienne has already been in some precarious situations up to now, this is a completely new experience – both for her herself and the viewer.

Up to now, we have only known her as a brave and ruthless warrior who more or less quickly disposes of her opponents. Imminent rape, though, catapults her into an almost hopeless position...

Brienne's bloodcurdling cries for help clearly do not leave Jaime as unmoved as he previously, pretentiously announced as she is eventually dragged away, kicked and punched in the pit of her stomach, despite her struggles. Since, after all, these cries ultimately encourage him to act:

With an invented story regarding the "Sapphire Isle" of Tarth, Brienne's homeland, and the associated prospects of vast quantities of gemstones should she be returned to her father Selwyn untouched, which completely convinces Locke, he is able to entice his captor and save his companion from her tormentors. The same woman who he persistently, savagely irritated and humiliated in the past and who basically did not really matter to him.

Personally, I think that it was not just Brienne's frightened cries that made him react. He may well have seen an opportunity to return the favor to the woman for the rescue from the three Northmen. Being in Brienne's custody with the prospect of soon seeing his father and, above all, his sister again would have presumably been the far more pleasant alternative to what the three Stark men might have done to him. It is just too bad that he carelessly risked everything...

However, there could also be other considerations behind this which I will return to in chapter 3.04.

With this move, it dawns on Jaime that Locke clearly seems to be corrupted, and thus he promises him perpetual wealth should he also be returned to his father.

When he eventually begins to boast more and more about the influence and fortunes of his family and considers the war for the North to be hopeless, Locke agrees with him and gives Jaime the impression that he is like-minded.

A fatal misconception and the beginning of Jaime's personal catastrophe...

Under the pretext of wanting to serve him food and the astonished glances from Brienne, who is obviously questioning what is actually going on, Locke removes Jaime's shackles, but only to shortly thereafter show him with a first-class demonstration of power that neither his father nor his gold can help him here and now.

("You're nothing without your daddy, and your daddy ain't here."). Because right here and now it's Locke who calls the shots.

Without warning, the man-at-arms sworn to House Bolton chops Jaime's right hand off with one powerful stroke of his meat knife and thus makes it brutally clear to the Kingslayer what he thinks of his arrogant talk.

Not only does Jaime lose his sword hand forever. The hand that made him what he is or was: one of the best swordsmen in Westeros... No. With this stroke, Locke also leaves the viewer behind as if hit by a wrecking ball, before the end credits roll under the thumping sounds of the punk-rock version of "The Bear and the Maiden Fair" by the US indie rock band "The Hold Steady" and Jaime's painful scream, thus reinforcing the already existing state of shock.

Episode 3.04
And Now His Watch is Ended

The following day (and on the way back to Robb Stark it seems), Jaime, who is exhausted from his mutilation, is subjected to offensive humiliations from the Northmen.

When the Kingslayer, drained of all his powers, eventually falls from his saddle into the mud and asks for something to drink, the harassment continues with Locke initially pouring water over his head amidst the loud laughter of his men and then gives him horse urine to drink.

While Jaime is able to steal a sword from one of his tormentors despite his desolate situation, he has almost no chance with his untrained left hand. Thus, it is easy for the men to disarm him and kick him in the mud.

Brienne watched this drama unfold from a distance while sitting on her horse the whole time. She knows how it feels to be subjected to humiliation and makes a decision. Despite his constant insults towards her since Catelyn Stark sent them both off to King's Landing, despite his attempt to kill her in a duel and despite her bound hands, she leaps from her horse to come to the aid of her companion.

However, I do not think that this is exclusively due to Brienne's heartfelt sympathy which is repeatedly reflected in her facial expression and allows her to close her eyes from what she is forced to see. The oath that she made to Lady Stark to bring the Kingslayer to the capital and to trade him for the Stark girls there also certainly plays a decisive role, even if he is no longer completely unscathed. Nevertheless, her restraints and the numerical superiority of the opponents, who keep her in check with drawn swords, force her to abandon her plan.

The truly amazing thing about this is that, after leaping from her horse and regardless of her shackles, she is able to simply push two Bolton men aside like human-sized stuffed animals and she is only forced to give up due to unequal conditions. Nonetheless, this act illustrates how much energy and dynamism this woman has, and one may ask oneself what would have happened under fair conditions...

While Brienne is then pushed back to her horse, Locke gives Jaime, who is still lying in the mud and completely exhausted, a final warning not to do anything like that again in the future.

Location:
in the woods west of Rushing Falls, Riverlands

uring the following night camp, Brienne attempts to motivate Jaime, who is mentally broken and feeling worthless due to his mutilation, to not give up despite his situation.

Yet, the man who was famous and notorious for his sword hand, which was taken from him forever by Locke the previous night, is almost unresponsive to Brienne's efforts to awaken his spirits.

He only shows signs of life once when she quite insensitively describes his loss as a "misfortune".

Even though Brienne meant to be motivating and in no way disparaging, her choice of words evokes Jaime's outrage in the form of a vicious and angry remark ("Misfortune? I was that hand!"). Her very direct manner beautifully reflects her inexperience in dealing with other people. In any case, this must sound like a farce or mockery to Jaime since his companion apparently completely underestimates the importance of his sword hand.

"You have a taste, one taste of the real world where people have important things taken from them, and you whine and cry and quit. You sound like a bloody woman!"
- **Brienne to Jaime Lannister**

With her almost philosophical and slightly inciting attempt to explain that the loss of his hand is anything but fair and that he must not behave girlishly and give up completely, she tries to save the situation, but Jaime does not comment on this. He also cannot or will not answer when she asks him what made him not only protect her from abuse but also probably save her life with his (invented) story the night before.

I have already speculated as to why Jaime ultimately saved Brienne from rape in the corresponding chapter. It may have been the thought of his once sworn knightly oath to protect the innocent. Perhaps he finally realized that his escape attempt on the bridge was completely foolish because it was how he put himself and Brienne in this position. Or maybe he does not want to suffer the ignominy of admitting that this woman now means something to him and he secretly admires her perseverance and discipline.

Of course, I can only offer presumptions in this respect. It is impossible to determine what actually drove his behavior. Probably a little bit of everything...

Kissed by Fire

Location:
Harrenhal, Riverlands

ontrary to expectations, Brienne and Jaime are not brought to Robb Stark but to Harrenhal, a huge castle almost destroyed by dragon fire in the Riverlands, where they are received by Roose Bolton, the Lord of the Dreadfort and leader of House Bolton.

On his way from Oxcross to the South, Robb Stark, among others, stopped in Harrenhal. He ceded control of the castle to Roose Bolton, one of the most loyal Stark vassals, so that he could ultimately attend the funeral of his grandfather Hoster Tully.

Despite all of the hostility between the Lannisters and the North, Roose Bolton shows Jaime respect. The Lord of the Dreadfort especially apologizes to Brienne for the improper behavior from his men ("Apologies, my lady. You're under my protection now.") and at least loosens some of her shackles. Even if the Northman is polite to her in these circumstances, Brienne's facial expression alone demonstrates a great deal of (due?) skepticism towards him.

When he asks for news from the capital, Jaime learns from Lord Bolton that Stannis Baratheon has now laid siege to and attacked King's Landing. However, the attack could eventually be repelled with the help of his father Tywin's troops. When the Bolton leader continues and tells him that his sister Cersei is well, Jaime falls to the ground in both relief and exhaustion.

| Location: |
| **Harrenhal, Riverlands** |

When Brienne is allowed to have a hot bath in the castle's bathhouse and, to her surprise, Jaime is standing in front of her, the blonde woman is not too keen on having to share a tub with him.

Of all the men in the world, the Kingslayer would probably have been the last man she would have wanted to show herself completely naked to. It is understandable that she tries to place as much possible distance between herself and her uninvited guest.

Like a shy deer and with her typical, suspicious look as if to say, "keep away from me", she shamefully cowers in the furthest corner since Jaime almost incessantly irritated and demeaned her wherever he could. And despite his state of exhaustion, he cannot help himself but offend Brienne by provocatively stepping into her tub, even though other tubs are free.

Up until this point, I found Brienne to be "simply" likable and sympathetic and that it would be a shame if this character were to be killed off in the near future. This almost legendary bathhouse sequence or, to be precise, the two key scenes within the bathhouse plot, managed to ultimately make this "simply" sympathetic and yet extraordinary character my favorite one within a few minutes.

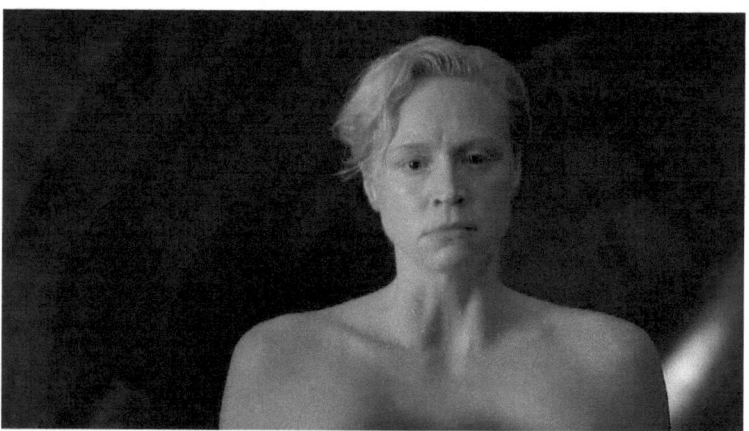

The first of these two key scenes takes place right at the beginning, once Jaime has made himself comfortable opposite Brienne, when he mocks her for failing as protector for the second time after Renly's murder ("You're supposed to get me back to King's Landing in one piece. Not going so well, is it? No wonder Renly died with you guarding him."), and she jumps out of the water as if stung by an adder. This look full of dislike and anger when she then towers over Jaime at a height of over six feet and her deeply offended "Don't you mock me" statement make it clear how crude and incorrect his accusations towards her are – simply staggering!

However, the truly noteworthy thing in this scene is that Brienne's otherwise enormous feeling of shame appears to have completely disappeared when she shows herself entirely naked to the Kingslayer, only to defend her deeply wounded pride.

This is a really interesting aspect regarding her maxim!

The resoluteness in her look and words then causes an arrogant Jaime Lannister to ask her for forgiveness for his hurtful words after a brief period of silence and reflection. He knows that he was wrong to blame her for Renly's death, even though he does not know the exact circumstances that led to his murder. But he knows that she adored him beyond all measure. It is also clear to him that she is not to blame for his mutilation, but he himself is to blame since he infuriated Locke with his dreadful talk. The word "thanks" does not pass his lips, but he at least tells her that he would probably not be alive without her ("That was unworthy. Forgive me. You protected me better than most.").

To calm the situation in the long term, Jaime proposes a "truce" between him and Brienne.

Indeed, the woman accepts the proposal with typical skepticism, though she has earned the required trust from him. After all, he has proved anything but trustworthy to date.

Without being asked by Brienne, Jaime then begins to tell her about the day King's Landing was sacked from his point of view, when King Aerys II. Targaryen, the "Mad

King", fell victim to the rebellion and ultimately his, Jaime's, sword. Since then, the nickname Kingslayer has stuck to him like an ulcer that cannot be removed.

Slightly annoyed and disinterested at first, Brienne becomes more and more spellbound by Jaime's speech the further he progresses with the story of what unfolded.

When he eventually, quite provocatively confronts her with the question of whether she would have kept her oath to Renly if he had ordered her to kill her own father, like Aerys did to Jaime, Brienne cannot find an answer. Instead, swallowing hard, she stares at her counterpart with her mouth half open and round-eyed like a little girl who has heard an almost unbelievable-sounding story from her father. This facial expression was simply compelling, and it was her second aforementioned reaction that downright overwhelmed me.

After the encounter with the farmer in *Dark Wings, Dark Words* (Episode 3.02), Jaime plunges Brienne into emotional chaos in relation to the subject of oaths for the second time ... and again she has no answer for him.

Towards the end of his speech, it becomes clear to the gripped Brienne that she did not know the true background to the title, Kingslayer, although it is true that Jaime's action, which ultimately gave him this derogatory nickname, should in no way be seen as morally reprehensible in this particular case, and thus this condemnation only takes the overall circumstances into consideration to a limited extent.

Visibly troubled by the hardships in his story and weakened by his wound, Jaime eventually collapses into the woman's arms.

When Brienne catches him, it becomes clear that he has a great deal of trust in her. She previously demanded this trust from him when he told her that he no longer wanted to argue and before he started recounting the events from over seventeen years ago from his point of view.

Instead, she could have allowed him to simply pass out and drown in the tub.

Jaime now finally seems willing to not only accept this woman but also to respect and look out for her.

When Jaime is lying exhausted in her arms, it is wonderful to see and, above all, hear him correct Brienne and explain that it is not the Kingslayer who needs help, but rather Jaime ("Jaime. My name is Jaime.") as she calls for the guards.

Incidentally, "Kingslayer" is the title of the somewhat melancholic piece that brilliantly captures the moment and can be heard very softly in the background.

The Climb

Location: **Harrenhal, Riverlands**

Tastes obviously differ, and it appears that Roose Bolton's men have not yet encountered Brienne's style with regard to her pink dress. However, I believe that the color is the lesser of the evils...

She feels distinctly uneasy and perhaps a little vulnerable without her armor in such an accentuated feminine garment, and when her host, Lord Bolton, says that his men have finally found her something appropriate to wear at the beginning of their meal together, simply the manner of her reply, "Yes. Most kind of them", reveals that she is only wearing it out of mere courtesy.

Brienne's immediately expressed justification that she was simply following Catelyn Stark's order with her (failed) mission promptly encounters heavy resistance from Roose Bolton. He informs her in an abrasive tone that

Catelyn Stark has already been arrested by her son for treason and that she was only saved from execution because she is his mother.

It seems that the trust between Brienne and Jaime that slowly emerged in the bathhouse has continued when she eventually puts an end to his unsuccessful efforts to cut his meat into mouth sized pieces with one hand by using her fork to replace his missing hand. It obviously mattered to Brienne that her fellow sufferer was starving next to her. And Jaime himself would not have allowed anyone who he did not at least feel a tiny amount of sympathy for to simply poke around with his food without objection.

The following sequence also provides another fine example of this aforementioned sympathy when Lord Bolton tells his involuntary guests that it would probably be safest for him to kill them both and dispose of their corpses rather than returning them to the King in the North, and not be held accountable by Jaime's father for his fealty to the Starks. Irritated by this subtle and provocative remark, Brienne reaches for her cutlery knife but is prevented from possibly doing something thoughtless by Jaime who immediately senses her thoughts and calmingly places his hand on hers.

I am sure that these reciprocal reactions would have been completely unthinkable a few days ago. Thank goodness for the spa area in Harrenhal!

Despite the fact that he is a committed Stark vassal, Roose Bolton then declares himself willing to allow Jaime to go to King's Landing and not to send him back to Robb Stark which comes as a surprise to Jaime.

The Lord of the Dreadfort is certainly aware of the value of his hostage. In this respect, this does not seem to be due to the prospect of the generous reward promised to him by

Jaime should he be returned to his father, or the fear of Tywin's retaliation should he not return Jaime or kill him instead.

In fact, Lord Bolton would like to gain the favor of the Lannisters in case of the defeat of the North and not to stand on the losing side at the end. And a defeat seems absolutely realistic at present since the Karstarks have now broken their allegiance with the Starks as one of the larger noble houses in the North following the execution of their leader.

After the Kingslayer murdered Rickard Karstark's son, Torrhen, during his escape from Robb Stark's camp, his father demanded swift retaliation after Jaime's recapture, which Catelyn Stark denied him, as is well known.

She put Brienne on a secret mission to bring Jaime Lennister to the capital to trade him for her daughters there for fear that the Kingslayer could still fall victim to the upset father. Angered by ultimately being robbed of his vengeance, Lord Karstark later murdered two of Jaime Lannister's nephews, who were being held prisoner by the Northmen, as scapegoats behind Robb Stark's back. This is why Robb personally executed the Lord of Karhold for treason.

The Karstarks thereupon turned away from the King in the North.

However, Jaime must continue his journey south alone because, in contrast to him, Brienne is charged with abetting treason and must stay in Harrenhal by order of Lord Bolton...

Episode 3.07

The Bear and the Maiden Fair

Location:
Harrenhal, Riverlands

n the evening before his departure, Jaime once again visits Brienne in her chamber, which serves her as a cell, to bid her farewell.

She is surprised to see him still in Harrenhal since she believed he would actually already be on his way towards King's Landing.

Brienne senses trouble when Jaime tells her that he will leave Harrenhal the next day, as well as Roose Bolton, who accepts an invitation to Edmure Tully's wedding at the Twins but she should remain behind in Harrenhal with Locke.

If the Bolton man-at-arms can suddenly cut off the Kingslayer's hand without batting an eyelid, what would he do with her, a woman? Nevertheless, she would not like Jaime to remember her moaning or downhearted but rather with her head held high and proud...

Contrary to Robb Stark's agreement with Walder Frey to marry one of his daughters/granddaughters because he allowed Robb and his troops to pass the Twins as a crossing over the Green Fork of the Trident at that time, Robb took Talisa Maegyr as his wife.

Concerned about a possible act of revenge by Walder Frey against his family, Robb's uncle Edmure Tully, Catelyn's younger brother, eventually agrees to settle this debt. Incidentally, this consideration is not entirely without reason since Walder Frey is extremely resentful. He has always felt disrespected by the Tullys as his feudal lords and he is anything but sympathetic to them.

"When Catelyn Stark released you, we both made a promise to her. Now it's your promise. You gave your word. Keep it and consider the debt paid."
- **Brienne to Jaime Lannister**

In the firm belief that her journey is most likely now over and she would no longer be able to keep her promise to Catelyn Stark to bring her daughters to safety, she reminds Jaime that he gave his word and imposes the burden on him that he alone must fulfil the associated duty for both of them.

Her almost majestic look and the determination and calmness in her voice in the moment when she reminds Jaime of his promise to bring the Stark girls back home, is what I find incredibly moving in this scene.

And so he does. In return, Jaime gives Brienne his word that he will bring the Stark daughters back to their mother. With a heavy heart, he eventually bids farewell to his companion who acknowledges his words with a short nod and whom he must leave to an unknown fate.

Brienne's storyline is a true source of genuinely fascinating and moving moments. The following farewell scene is such a moment, when, despite her obvious efforts to compose herself and not let her true feelings show, she ultimately struggles to sadly say "Goodbye, Ser Jaime", and he appears to want to respond but he hesitates. Perhaps because he does not know what to say or because he does not dare to tell her that she means something to him.

Like in the scene where Brienne swears her loyalty to Catelyn Stark in the Kingswood, Ramin Djawadi's score of "The Old Gods and the New" can be heard in the background. This musical piece always manages to create an unbelievably intense and emotional atmosphere in these quite special "Brienne" scenes.

Incidentally, it is the first time that Brienne not only calls Jaime something other than Kingslayer but also addresses him according to his rank as "Ser" and his first name "Jaime". Thus, he hears exactly what he asked her for when he laid in her arms in the bathhouse. This demonstrates that Brienne now also appears to feel something for the man who humiliated her day in and day out.

The next day, Jaime sets off from Harrenhal to the South together with Qyburn, a former maester of the Citadel, who was deprived of his status some time ago due to prohibited experiments on living people, as his medical aid as well as a number of Bolton vassals as escorts.

However, in the courtyard of the destroyed fortress, Locke does not miss the chance to subtly point out that Jaime need not worry about his companion and that he will "take good care" of her....

Unfortunately for her, Locke's devious sounding turn of phrase to Jaime seems to increasingly confirm Brienne's hunch that he would mean nothing but trouble for her. And since Roose Bolton has also already set off towards the Twins, it seems that there is no one around who would be able to stop the Bolton man from any underhandedness. There may be real reason for Brienne to fear...

uring a rest break on the way to King's Landing, Qy-burn tends to Jaime's unhealed stump.

Upon his enquiry, the former maester tells him that Brienne's father offered Locke 300 gold dragons for her safe return. An offer which Jaime finds extremely fair. Unlike Locke who feels cheated out of the sapphires mentioned by Jaime and therefore declines it.

To be honest, I do not know how much 300 gold dragons converts to in today's money... but a few zeros are missing, right? Seven to eight? However, since Jaime is of the opinion that it is a reasonable price for Brienne, I would hope that this is the case. For who is more familiar with gold than a Lannister?

Jaime's prattle about the Tarth sapphires apparently aroused Locke's desire for the gemstones to such an extent that he now wants a big piece of the cake. But the Bolton man-at-arms does not have the IQ or the erudition of Jaime's brother Tyrion. Thus, he does not know that Tarth is not named the "Sapphire Isle" because of its sapphire mines but rather because of the sapphire blue water surrounding the island. Jaime would certainly not have been able to dupe his small-statured brother this way.

Feeling guilty and close to despair for possibly putting Brienne's life in danger with the tale he fed Locke at that time and also feeling pressured by Qyburn's claim that the Bolton men would probably do something terrible to her in the evening, Jaime warns Walton, one of the men charged with escorting him to King's Landing, to return to Harrenhal. But the man refuses to comply with Jaime's request.

Thus, Jaime presents the overburdened Bolton man with an almost hopeless situation: either receive a reward in King's Landing as a hero or be executed as his tormentor who Jaime would blame for the loss of his right hand.

Until recently, the fate of the Maiden of Tarth would probably have been irrelevant to Jaime. The fact that he then moves heaven and earth, and ultimately uses a ploy to save Brienne from a gruesome fate, is another unmistakable sign that the relationship between the two has fundamentally changed.

The small group then makes its way back to Harrenhal at a gallop...

Location:
Harrenhal, Riverlands

 ack in Harrenhal, Jaime finds that his concerns for Brienne were more than justified.

Armed only with a wooden sword, presumably *sarcasm bell ringing* to ensure equal opportunities, the woman is forced to fight against a fully-grown bear in a pit for the sheer pleasure of the men, including Locke, who are watching, jeering and singing the atmospheric and absolutely fitting "The Bear and the Maiden Fair".

The man-at-arms is surprised to see the Kingslayer again so soon but sees no reason to end the spectacle with the bear, no matter what price Jaime offers him.

Despite his handicap, which makes rescuing the woman seem almost impossible, and with confidence in the loyalty of the men who were commissioned by Roose Bolton to bring him to the capital, Jaime plucks up his courage and jumps into the arena to rescue Brienne.

While Jaime's return to Harrenhal alone deserves respect, he downright demonstrates his nobility by jumping into the bear pit to rescue Brienne and the related fact that he risked his own life for her.

However, as honorable and heroic as his efforts to save the blonde woman from a brutal fate may be, Jaime really pushed his luck. His struggles would have been doomed to failure, particularly if the men who were commissioned to bring him to King's Landing had not made every effort to rescue him (and ultimately also Brienne) from the bear. Thus, Jaime simply and grippingly played on the men's fear of Lord Bolton who would not allow this disregard of his instructions to go unpunished...

His plan is successful. The bear is distracted for a brief moment by bolts fired at it from Walton's crossbow. Jaime and Brienne, who are in extreme danger, use this fleeting moment to be pulled up by the crowd out of the arena onto the wooden palisade away from the furious animal.

However, Locke is still not willing to allow his reward in the form of Brienne to simply escape. Only when Jaime in turn makes it clear that he would die before continuing his journey without the woman, something that would certainly not be in the interest of Lord Bolton and could probably cost Locke his head, the verbally cornered man-at-arms agrees to let the woman go to the capital.

Brienne's furious glance at the Bolton man for his insidious game when she passes him without saying a word is remarkable. No triumphant gesture, no joy - just contempt.

However, despite all the euphoria about Jaime's selfless rescue operation, one should also keep in mind that he was essentially cleaning up the mess he caused previously with a few ill-considered statements, and one can now analyze the possible reasons as to why Jaime returned to Harrenhal.

For me personally, the increased and honestly felt sympathy towards Brienne plays a very crucial role in this respect: without this sympathy, he certainly would not have had the guilty conscience for her predicament which was already mentioned in the previous scene. And without this affection, he probably would not have visited the woman to bid her farewell before departing from Harrenhal. Consequently, his knightly oath regarding the girls would have never existed.

Whatever the real reason was, it is really interesting to see how Jaime appears to turn over a new leaf, and it is great that Brienne played a major role in this positive development.

Episode 3.10
Mhysa

Location:
**King's Landing, capital of the Seven Kingdoms,
Crownlands**

Together with Qyburn, Brienne and Jaime eventually reach the capital undetected without further incidents.

When Jaime accidentally bumps into a roadman, who then deprecatingly calls him "country boy", it suggests that he really is not recognized as he once was.

Once he was the Kingslayer in the shining armor of the Kingsguard, who could command respect from everyone, well... at least as far as his sword skills were concerned. Now he is just one more unkempt, humiliated and mutilated man clothed in rags whose only outstanding talent has been taken away from him.

Brienne's compassionate look to him during this brief incident speaks for itself. Similar to the degradation that

Jaime had to experience from the Bolton men after his mutilation (Episode 3.04 *And Now His Watch is Ended*), she can at least sympathize to some extent with how things look from his perspective. Even if, unlike Jaime, she has no visible "reminder", the atrocities against her in the form of attempted rape and the "dance" with the bear were not half bad. Not to mention the insults suffered daily.

A Review of Season Three

This season is still my absolute favorite to date. Why do I specifically like this season, in which Brienne is almost continuously imprisoned with the exception of the first episode in which she appears and thus she has a significantly restricted sphere of action, so much? Well, the answer is really quite simple: it seems to me that this rather slower season is like a great test for her.

Extreme demands are placed on her here, both psychologically and physically, yet she must overcome all challenges without her proven tool, the sword, which is completely against her nature.

In my opinion, this season has plenty of magnificent scenes, where Jaime's sudden mutilation must certainly be regarded as the most shocking moment. Not just for him, but also for the viewer.

The events that ultimately lead to the finale with Brienne's rescue from Harrenhal are also excitingly showcased.

However, in this respect, it is primarily the quieter encounters between Jaime and Brienne in season three that I find truly magnificent. Above all, the famous bathhouse scene, in which mutual trust is shown for the first time after many quarrels, when Brienne finally holds her exhausted counterpart in her arms. An incredibly well staged intimate play that was ultimately decisive for the fact that I have grown to love Brienne so much.

The separation scene between Jaime and Brienne in Harrenhal represents another emotional highlight of this season for me. This essentially amplifies what already became clear in the bathhouse and reveals to the viewer something that goes beyond mere respect and admiration for the other - mutual sympathy.

Above all, Brienne's positive influence on Jaime's character and mindset is increasingly noticeable over the course of the season. What other reason would he have had to rescue her from attempted rape or the bear pit if a certain level of affection had not developed in him in the meantime? Overall, it is a truly superb storyline that shows Brienne in an unfamiliar role far from being able to control and take things into her own hands.

Season Four

Two Swords

| Location: |
| King's Landing, capital of the Seven Kingdoms, Crownlands |

Brienne visits Margaery Tyrell in the gardens of the Red Keep, who is in the process of preparing for her upcoming wedding to King Joffrey Baratheon together with her grandmother Olenna, and asks her for a private discussion.

Following Renly Baratheon's death, Petyr Baelish managed to forge an alliance between House Lannister and Tyrell. In return for the support of the Tyrells in the victorious Blackwater battle against Stannis Baratheon, King Joffrey agreed to marry Loras' sister Margaery.

Brienne's encounter with Olenna Tyrell demonstrates how difficult it is for her to deal with personal praise and recognition.

When she is greeted by Margaery's grandmother, who tells her about the rumors she heard about her, including the tournament victory against her grandson Loras ("We've heard all about you. But hearing is one thing. Aren't you just marvellous! Absolutely singular. (…) I hear you knocked my grandson into the dirt, like the silly little boy he is."), Brienne feels embarrassed and extremely self-conscious.

It is difficult for someone like Brienne, who is used to nothing but mockery and hostility, to suddenly deal with honest praise. Thus, her reaction is slightly awkward but also absolutely understandable from her point of view.

She politely ignores this statement and quickly changes the subject by persuading Margaery to take a stroll with her. The tall woman finally has the opportunity to tell Renly's widow the actual circumstances that led to her husband's murder.

In this respect, Brienne reaffirms to Margaery her vow to take revenge on Stannis Baratheon.

However, she makes a small verbal blunder when she describes Renly as "our" King. Without seeing this as a deliberate affront, the prospective Queen promptly and calmly corrects the slightly awkward woman by telling her that Joffrey is now the new King.

Brienne's deep attachment to Renly can still be heard here. She certainly knows that many things have changed in recent times. She also knows that the current King is named Joffrey and not Renly. Nevertheless, it seems that the thought that Renly is the one true King has been burned into her memory to such an extent that this statement came out unconsciously. Fortunately, Margaery is intelligent enough to not treat this statement as treason.

Wearing her blue culotte dress with a brown leather jerkin, Brienne can be seen without her obligatory armor for the first time (following the small fashion faux pas by the Boltons in Harrenhal) and in an outfit that is unusual for both her and the viewer but appropriate for the occasion.

| Location: |
| **King's Landing, capital of the Seven Kingdoms, Crownlands** |

During a subsequent conversation between Brienne and Jaime, who has now been appointed Lord Commander of the Kingsguard despite his handicap, there is slight dissonance about his promise to bring the two Stark girls to safety.

In Jaime's view, the whole situation has been considerably complicated by Catelyn Stark's murder, Arya Stark's probable death since she has not been seen since her father's execution and the wedding between her sister Sansa and his brother Tyrion. Therefore, he does not consider himself in a position or obliged to do something to that effect. An assessment Brienne does not agree with at all.

"Look me in the eye and tell me that you think she'll be safe in King's Landing." - **Brienne to Jaime Lannister**

Robb Stark went back on the agreement to marry one of the Frey girls and instead married Talisa Maegyr, an exotic foreigner from Volantis. Concerned about a possible act of revenge from Walder Frey, who was offended and resentful about Robb breaking his word, Robb's uncle Edmure Tully, Catelyn's younger brother, eventually agreed to settle this debt, albeit reluctantly.

At the subsequent wedding between Edmure and Roslyn Frey at the Twins, Walder Frey and Roose Bolton, in alliance with the Lannisters, conspired against their respective feudal lords, the Tullys and the Starks.

They orchestrated a massacre in which the King in the North, Robb Stark, his pregnant wife Talisa and his mother Catelyn were slaughtered among others. This massacre would gain notoriety as "The Red Wedding".

Following the imprisonment of her father Eddard, Arya Stark hid herself in King's Landing for some time. She had to watch as he was ultimately executed for treason and she fled the capital by dressing as a boy and joining a trek taking new recruits for the Brotherhood of the "Night's Watch" to the Wall (brief explanations of terms will follow later). She has been regarded as missing ever since.

After the engagement between Joffrey and Sansa Stark was broken off because the young King refused to marry the daughter of the traitor Eddard Stark, the girl remained at court in King's Landing as a hostage. Nevertheless, Tywin Lannister quickly married his son Tyrion to the eldest Stark daughter to secure the North for the Lannisters.

"(...) That makes Sansa Stark the heir to Winterfell. (...) You will wed her, bed her and put a child in her. (...) Sansa Stark is a finer reward than you could ever dare hope for. And it is past time you were wed."
Tywin Lannister to his son Tyrion (Episode 3.05 *Kissed by Fire*)

In contrast to her conversation partner, Brienne does not want to know anything about other circumstances. She still considers the girls to be in danger and thus their joint oath has not yet ended.

This scene is another very good example of how concerned Brienne is about fulfilling her moral duty and how she also demands this of others (Jaime in this case).

Annoyed by Brienne's stubbornness and feeling coerced into giving his word that Sansa is safe in the capital, knowing full well that he cannot guarantee this to her, Jaime ultimately unloads his frustration through old habits that she hoped had been forgotten by again targeting her appearance despite their developed relationship of trust ("Are you sure we're not related? Ever since I've returned, every Lannister I've seen has been a miserable pain in my ass. Maybe you're a Lannister, too. You've got the hair for it, if not the looks.").

A knee-jerk reaction with which he leaves a stunned Brienne without saying goodbye, who must feel like she has been hit in the face with a sledgehammer.

The Lion and the Rose

Location:
King's Landing, capital of the Seven Kingdoms, Crownlands

Brienne is also invited to the wedding celebrations of King Joffrey and Queen Margaery.

However, it is evident from the beginning of the scene that she has not immersed herself in life at court despite her noble origin, and she has problems with status-specific customs when she politely pays her respects to the bride and groom: instead of formally curtsy as you would expect from a Lady, Brienne bows like a man before the newlyweds, which is immediately noticed and smugly commented on by Joffrey's mother Cersei on the neighboring table.

Brienne feels embarrassed by her awkwardness and promptly tries to formally excuse her behavior ("Apologies, Your Grace. I never did master the curtsy.").

It is quite astounding that this woman can ride a horse and wield a sword like no other, and bending the knee before Renly and Catelyn Stark was without incident, too, but a formal curtsy is beyond her talent. Oh, well...

Despite this small mistake, she is greeted by the bride in an extremely friendly manner. When Joffrey goes to express his gratitude to her for killing one of his fiercest opponents, Renly Baratheon, the young King is immediately corrected by his wife who tells him that Renly was not killed by Brienne's hand.

At this point it becomes obvious that Margaery had no doubts (if she ever had any at all) about Brienne's declaration that she had nothing to do with Renly's death. However, Joffrey is grieved that Brienne is not the woman he expected to thank for Renly's death and he expresses his disappointment to her in a rather uncharming way ("A shame. I'd knight the man that put an end to that deviant's life.").

He is certainly unaware that Brienne is deeply hurt by his words. But even if he had been aware of her relationship to the deceased, I think that Joffrey would have made a disrespectful comment at best. More could not have been expected.

Well-mannered as Brienne is, she ignores his insulting and degrading words in an embarrassed manner, like she did previously in another context with Olenna Tyrell (Episode 4.01 *Two Swords*), and kindly commends the two.

When she is about to move away from the bridal couple, Brienne is stopped by Joffrey's mother, Cersei, who would like to thank her for the safe return of her brother Jaime.

Cersei's initial friendliness to Brienne including her statement that she holds the title of "Lady" because of her noble origin alone, whether she likes it or not, brings back Brienne's embarrassment as we have seen a few times in comparable situations.

However, Cersei is not someone who will engage in such a conversation without ulterior motives, and when Brienne tells her in a friendly way and without suspicion that Jaime actually saved her life more times than vice versa, the Queen Mother gets the (perhaps already feared) feeling that there is possibly far more between her brother and the blonde woman than the sheer will to help the other.

This is an assumption that she has to check. Is this female stranger to Cersei actually coming between her and Jaime?

Cersei's perceptible jealousy eventually culminates into a biting attack on Brienne where she accuses her of fickle loyalty and a form of mercenary mentality to only serve people who appeal to her – including her brother Jaime.

Although the tall woman vehemently denies the last point ("I don't serve your brother, Your Grace!"), her facial expression and, above all, the seconds of speechlessness when she hears Cersei's provocative remark that she may not serve her brother but she loves him, give the impression that she has been caught in relation to her feelings.

Since she is far more skillful with the sword than with words and quick-wittedness is not exactly one of her strengths, she leaves Cersei with a simple "Your Grace" and goes on her way.

Episode 4.03

Breaker of Chains

Location:
King's Landing, capital of the Seven Kingdoms, Crownlands

King Joffrey has been murdered – and at his own wedding! Apparently, he was poisoned by his short-statured uncle and Cersei's youngest brother, Tyrion.

Although the mother of the murdered King has Tyrion seized immediately by members of the Kingsguard, Tyrion's wife Sansa has suddenly vanished from the face of the earth. And she really would have had sufficient reason to murder Joffrey, even if she was apparently not actively involved in the act.

After Joffrey had Sansa's father, Eddard Stark, beheaded as a traitor before her eyes, he later forced her to look at his impaled head on the city wall. He also repeatedly humiliated Sansa, who was held hostage in King's Landing since then, and he allowed Ser Meryn Trant, Joffrey's personal bodyguard, to mistreat her as a female "scapegoat" for her brother Robb's successful battles.

Brienne only briefly appears in this scene from afar and from behind (almost exactly below center screen) among the horrified wedding guests. She does not have an active role in this scene, nor is she the topic of conversation for other characters. Nevertheless, I have included this scene in my review because the name of her actress is listed in the opening credits as so-called "credit only".

Thus, Brienne witnesses Joffrey's murder up close and also simultaneously learns of Sansa Stark's (now Lannister) disappearance...

Oathkeeper

Location:
King's Landing, capital of the Seven Kingdoms, Crownlands

The fact that Catelyn Stark is said to have simply released her brother Jaime at that time makes Cersei suspicious. She has him called to her chambers and demands an explanation from him.

In this respect, it is not only Jaime's diminishing loyalty to her or the royal house that she fears. It is primarily her brief conversation with Brienne that apparently evoked a strong feeling of jealousy in her when Brienne remained silent in response to Cersei's suggestive accusation that she loves her brother.

Why else would she disparagingly call the tall woman a "great cow" during her conversation with Jaime, even though the two only met at the wedding ceremony for the first time, if she did not consider her to be a serious rival?

Cersei reacts very indignantly to Jaime's honest answer to her initial question that he had sworn to Lady Stark to bring her daughters back if they are still alive. Nevertheless, she considers her expectations confirmed and accuses him of swearing an oath to the enemy, Catelyn Stark. But since Lady Stark is already dead and thus her brother is now free from any oaths or promises, she tests his devotion to her which she hopes still exists.

In a subtle way that is typical for her, she asks her brother to find and execute the "murderous little bitch" Sansa before her eyes...

Location:
King's Landing, capital of the Seven Kingdoms, Crownlands

In the private rooms of the Lord Commander of the Kingsguard, Jaime allows Brienne to read entries about him in the so-called "Book of Brothers" which records all the deeds of every knight who has ever served in the Kingsguard.

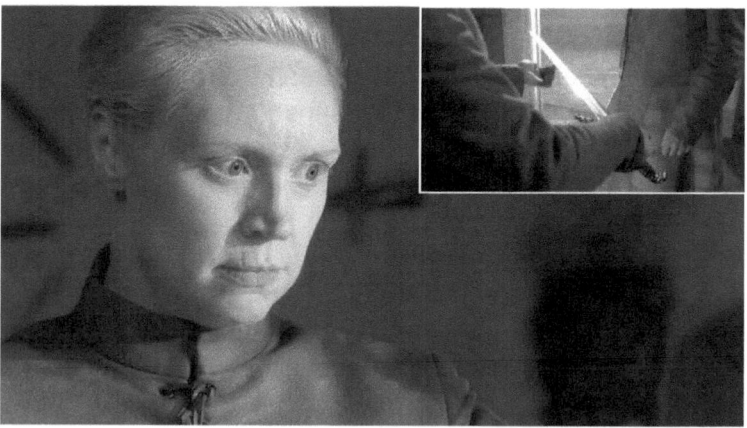

She seems touched as she reads the last sentence: "(...) Thereafter known as 'the Kingslayer'.". She knows from Jaime's account in Harrenhal that this name is anything but true, and it is noticeable how painful it is for her to read this passage so indiscriminately.

When Jaime gives her a sword made of Valyrian steel for no apparent reason that his father Tywin had reforged and gave to him after his return to the capital, Brienne is noticeably surprised and moved and she vehemently refuses to accept this noble and precious gift.

After Eddard Stark's execution, Tywin Lannister had his Valyrian steel long sword "Ice" melted down and reforged into two new swords. He gave one, the slightly smaller one, to his grandson Joffrey as a wedding gift. The other sword he presented to his son Jaime as an incentive to step down from the Kingsguard due to his handicap. Jaime refused to step down, but he kept the sword regardless.

Only Jaime's expressed wish ultimately persuades Brienne to accept the sword. Her hesitation is understandable. Over the years, she has become more accustomed to "gifts" in the form of mockery, rejection or insults.

Though it was somehow predictable that this generous thoughtfulness was not without a valid reason. Thus, Jaime once again reminds Brienne of their joint oath and explains to her that Ned Stark's steel was made for at least finding and protecting Sansa since he ultimately suggests that her younger sister, Arya, is already dead like her mother. With the sword, he places his hope in the hands of the woman and thus cleverly circumvents the moral conflict of wanting to keep his promise to Catelyn Stark and, above all, Brienne on the one hand, and following his sister's command on the other.

As if the sword was not appreciation enough, he puts Brienne on the spot again when he then presents her with new armor together with a corresponding tunic. Since her old one was removed when they were imprisoned by the Boltons, Jaime spares no expense and has new armor made in noble dark blue according to her measurements.

"I'll find her. For Lady Catelyn. And for you."
- **Brienne to Jaime Lannister**

Straight speechless and overwhelmed by all these gestures and sensing that he is placing a lot of confidence in her, she reaffirms her promise to Jaime that she will make every effort to find the girl (or perhaps girls) and will not let him or the already deceased Catelyn Stark down.

But he also has something else for her....

Location:
at the Gates to King's Landing, start of the Kingsroad, Crownlands

---

Or rather: someone else... Podrick Payne.
Soon after, however, when she is standing before Jaime and Tyrion's long-standing squire in her new armor, Brienne is not at all enthusiastic about the idea of travelling with a companion.

Even though this is probably the very first time she has seen the boy, she fears that he would be an additional burden for her. And the Maiden of Tarth really does not have the necessary patience or sufficient time to play nanny.

Jaime, though, insists that she takes him along as her squire since Podrick is no longer safe following Tyrion's arrest in the capital, and his small-statured brother finally owes him something.

During the Blackwater battle against Stannis Baratheon's troops, Podrick saved Tyrion's life by driving a lance through the back of Kingsguard Ser Mandon Moor's head when he tried to kill Tyrion. Since Tyrion was arrested for Joffrey's murder and there was a very close and familiar relationship between the Lord and squire (which still exists), Jaime fears that Podrick could also be accused of being a co-conspirator.

Even when Podrick witnesses Brienne's obvious reluctance towards him first hand, he makes no effort to decline the journey with her.

Why should he? Jaime's quite plausible statement that the capital is not a safe place for him and the prospect of travelling with a person who could offer him protection with her imposing appearance alone in the near future, seem to be sufficient reasons for the boy to humbly offer his services as squire. ("I won't slow you down, Ser. M-m-mylady. I promise I'll serve you well.").

There may be several reasons for the fact that he initially calls her "Ser", the title for a (male) knight, like a shy little boy and then quickly corrects his mistake but then stumbles over his words on the second attempt: on the one hand, because it is the first time serving a woman, and on the other, Brienne appears truly daunting and thus makes him nervous due to her stature.

She ultimately, reluctantly accepts Jaime's wish to take Podrick on her mission so as not to disappoint him.

While the boy immediately sets about saddling his Lady's horse, Jaime and Brienne face each other once again in a moving farewell scene like in Harrenhal (Episode 3.07 *The Bear and the Maiden Fair*).

It is almost characteristic for this woman that her answer to Jaime's question ("They say the best swords have names. Any ideas?") about a name for her sword is eventually "Oathkeeper" after some thinking.

Oathkeeper, a more appropriate name could not have been chosen.

Since, in contrast to King Joffrey, who destructively and menacingly named his swords "Hearteater" and "Widow's Wail", she almost solemnly affirms her longing desire and duty to keep her sworn oath to Catelyn Stark with this name as an everlasting reminder.

When Jaime acknowledges her choice with a quick approving nod and then bids her farewell with the words "Goodbye, Brienne.", she looks at him for a short moment, subtly nods her head and eventually walks around him to her horse without saying a word and close to tears.

This scene is virtually identical to the scene in Harrenhal, albeit in reverse. Back then, she bade him farewell, and so he does it to her this time. And there was no answer both times. But just like in the ruins in the Riverlands, Jaime once again lets Brienne go to face an uncertain future.

The coinciding, modified version of "The Old Gods and the New", which is slightly more powerfully arranged and highlighted with heavier beats, as well as Brienne's last look back to Jaime anxiously looking back at her, round off this really touching final sequence magnificently. It is a longing, sorrowful look. By now at the latest, the viewer should have no doubt that, despite her initial dislike to-wards him, with Jaime she appears to have found someone to whom she means just as much as he does to her, and whom she will possibly never see again.

His time with Brienne clearly appears to have been good for Jaime, and it is a real shame that they have to part ways again after such a short period of time.

First of His Name

Location:
Kingsroad near Brindlewood, Crownlands

Still annoyed by having to travel with an unwanted companion, Brienne tries with all her means to persuade Podrick to turn back to King's Landing and leave her.

"I've made it this far in the world without a squire. I don't see why I need one now." - **Brienne to Podrick Payne**

If, from the outset, she already had the feeling that Podrick would be a burden for her, rather than being useful to her, this impression is reinforced by the fact that he is barely able to keep his horse on a straight path, despite the leisurely pace. Thus, the prospects are not too bright for their forthcoming journey over a period of several weeks to Castle Black and Sansa's half-brother Jon, where Brienne believes Sansa may have been taken.

But Podrick displays a similar stubbornness as Brienne. Thus, her final attempt (for the time being) to get rid of him by releasing him from his oath to serve her also fails.

Where should the poor boy go, though? He does not have many alternatives. So, he is forced to continue letting Brienne's grumpy looks and snappy remarks wash over him.

Even this scene where Brienne is not exactly "ladylike" shows her honest, principled nature. She makes it quite clear to her companion that she does not want him, that she does not need him and she thinks he is completely unsuitable for her mission instead of putting up a brave front and secretly making her escape in the dark of night at the earliest opportunity and abandoning him to his own fate, as many others would perhaps do in her situation.

Location:
Woodlands south of Harrenhal near the Kingsroad, Riverlands

If Podrick's previous rather adventurous attempts to keep his horse on a straight path were understandable to a certain degree because he simply lacked experience, Brienne is horrified to learn that his culinary skills also have not come very far during a subsequent rest break when he tries to grill a rabbit over a fireplace without skinning it. By the way, this scene has a light slapstick character that always reminds me of a certain Mr. Bean...

Although Podrick tries to excuse his ineptness by saying that he was mainly a cupbearer for Lord Tyrion and not responsible for food preparation, it certainly does not take a star rated chef to know that the animal must be skinned before frying or grilling if you do not want to be left holding a flaming torch.

The boy senses that his approval ratings are constantly falling, and thus he sets about helping Brienne to remove her armor without being asked. Perhaps because he thinks he cannot do anything wrong in this respect...

Even though Podrick means well, Brienne strongly objects ("I've been removing my own armor for quite some time, thank you very much.") and makes it unmistakably clear that she does not need his help in that regard.

Another aspect may be the fact that she detests intimate closeness with a person who is still a stranger to her, and male at that.

While Brienne is in the process of loosening the buckles and straps of her armor, Podrick answers her question as to whether he has ever been in active combat.

He describes how he once saved the life of his former lord, Tyrion Lannister, by driving a lance through the back of a Kingsguard's head when he tried (presumably on the order of a third party) to kill his lord. This statement draws Brienne's attention, but she retains her typical skepticism.

Even if he is clearly of little value to her, it appears that Podrick at least has something akin to unconditional loyalty to his respective superior. At least she can be pleased about that.

When Brienne fails in her ongoing, desperate efforts to remove her armor, she eventually has no choice but to seek Podrick's assistance that she had previously vehemently rejected.

While a smile appears on the boy's face when she calls him to help her out of her dilemma with a stroppy "Help me with the straps!", her pained facial expression shows how much this concession frustrates her and dents her ego. One man's joy is another (wo)man's sorrow...

Mockingbird

Location: **Inn at the Crossroads, Riverlands**

Brienne hopes that it was just a one-off that Podrick had to help her remove her armor. She once again makes her dislike towards him known at the earliest opportunity during a break at the Inn at the Crossroads, a popular meeting point for travellers along the Kingsroad. She initially harps on about his unsuccessful food preparation in an unusually cynical manner for her circumstances ("We've been sleeping in ditches the last few weeks. I think we can treat ourselves to a featherbed for the night and a hot meal not cooked by you.") and then takes his beer mug out of his hand and abruptly warns him not to get drunk, like a mother looking after her young child, so that he does not do anything forbidden.

Curiously, Brienne, who should essentially know how it feels to suffer constant mockery from her own experience, deals with Podrick in almost the same manner. Furthermore, her only reason for this is to put him off the journey with her as quickly as possible. Bad girl!

Shortly thereafter, the two unintentionally make the acquaintance of the local barkeeper "Hot Pie", an orphan from Flea Bottom who ended up there in a roundabout way and simply goes by the name of his favorite meal as he is unaware of his real name.

When he sits down at the table with his guests without being asked, Brienne is less than enthusiastic about his obtrusiveness. Especially when he explains how to prepare a good kidney pie in great detail, you can tell this is something that the woman has always wanted to know by her annoyed expressions.

Upset and irritated by his subsequent probing questions about what led her to the Riverlands, Brienne eventually reveals that she is searching for Sansa Stark. A behavior that is rash but completely typical for this woman.

She appears unsuspicious and wastes no thought on whether she may be on thin ice by saying this to a complete stranger. Furthermore, all other guests in the room would have also heard her loud voice.

Under the pretext of not knowing the Starks and not wanting anything to do with traitors, Hot Pie abruptly ends the conversation.

"I pledged my life to their mother Catelyn Stark. I swore to her to bring her daughter home." - **Brienne to Hot Pie**

The tall woman is convinced that the boy clearly knows more than he is letting on but even the determined mention of her sworn oath to Catelyn Stark to bring her daughters to safety is unable to change his mind.

Before Brienne and Podrick go to their horses ready to depart the following morning, Hot Pie then surprisingly gives the two some interesting information, not about the mentioned Sansa but about her sister, Arya

Brienne had obviously convinced the barkeeper that she was someone who could be absolutely trusted with her intense and honest-sounding announcement the previous evening.

He tells the skeptical but attentively listening woman about his and Arya's joint odyssey since King's Landing, until they fell into the hands of the "Brotherhood without Banners", a group of outlaws who are committed to protecting the smallfolk on dubious grounds. They eventually parted ways when he was sold by the group to the local innkeeper, but Arya was to be brought to Riverrun in order to collect her ransom. The Brotherhood also had another prisoner in tow at the same time, a certain Sandor Clegane, who Podrick immediately recognizes as the "Hound", a former member of King Joffrey's Kingsguard who Podrick knows from his time as Tyrion's squire and who had to answer for various crimes committed by order of the Lannisters before the rebels…

When Arya Stark joined a trek taking new recruits for the Night's Watch to the Wall after the execution of her father, Hot Pie was also part of this "selected" group. However, they were captured by Lannister soldiers on the way north and taken to Harrenhal. Both of them were able to escape, but they were seized by the Brotherhood without Banners shortly after. While Hot Pie was then sold to the innkeeper of the Crossroads Inn, Arya was to be brought to Riverrun.

Hot Pie hereby dispels Podrick's fear that Brienne may have made a serious mistake by carelessly divulging information ("The Lannisters want Lady Sansa. The Lannisters have money. People kill for money. I don't think we should be telling people we're searching for Lady Sansa.") which he had previously expressed to Brienne.

This is probably a fear that the shy boy would preferably not have voiced and he only said it aloud upon Brienne's energetic demand. He ultimately did not want his words of criticism to make himself more unpopular with her than he already is. But his doubtful facial expression did not escape her attention.

Brienne's biting and almost humiliating reply ("You're not interesting enough to be offensive.") to Podrick's initial refusal to give her the reason for his not entirely unfounded discontent ("Don't want to offend. Truly. I don't."), is another fantastic demonstration of how little she thinks of him, to put it mildly.

The fact that, contrary to expectations, Hot Pie ultimately turned out to be a rich source of information gives Brienne the satisfaction of being proved right, unlike Podrick with his concerns. This is reason enough for her to outwardly celebrate this with a short, smirking grin and a triumphant "Um... You were saying?" to her squire.

*O*n their path towards the North, Podrick corrects the theory developed at the beginning of their journey, to head for Castle Black in the hope of finding Arya or Sansa there.

Since Walder Frey is now the new Lord of Riverrun by royal decree after the death of Catelyn Stark and her father Hoster Tully, only the Eyrie, the stronghold of House Arryn, could be considered a worthwhile destination for the Brotherhood. Lysa Arryn, Catelyn Stark's sister who is Arya and Sansa's last living relative, or more importantly for the Brotherhood, last living 'wealthy' relative, is currently living there.

Instead of continuing on the Kingsroad towards the North, the two turn eastward on the East Road towards the Vale of Arryn and the Eyrie.

Even if she refrains from admitting it and he is entirely incapable of many things in her eyes, Brienne must recognize that Podrick's knowledge about the political entanglements of the noble houses, who married into which house and who is enemies with whom, may be of great use.

After all, they had a long journey ahead, and it would have been a crying shame if they had made it the entire way to the Wall in vain just because such important information and the conclusions drawn from this information had slipped through their fingers.

The Children

Location:
**at the beginning 30, later 10 miles west of the "Bloody Gate",
Vale of Arryn**

$\mathcal{S}$ince he was able to impress with his concentrated knowledge about the political entanglements of noble houses, Podrick once again tries to restore Brienne's picture of him. Or, to put it vividly: he destroys his own handiwork again...

This time, since he failed to tether their two horses as shown by Brienne and thus the horses ran away overnight, the two must now continue their journey through the wasteland in the Vale of Arryn on foot. As punishment for his clumsiness, an irritated Brienne, confirmed in her opinion of Podrick, has him carry the saddlebags for the last 30 miles to the Eyrie. Poor Pod....

Some 20 miles later, the two encounter a young girl practicing her swordplay with her stiletto-like sword in the mountains. A pleasant and lively conversation initially develops between the two women in which it becomes clear that they have more in common than originally thought – the desire to be a warrior and a father who did not want or support this at first.

When the male companion of the girl finally appears, who Podrick immediately recognizes as Sandor Clegane, the Hound, Brienne remembers the information from Hot Pie that he was last seen with Arya Stark. Putting two and two together, she realizes that the girl must be Arya, one of the two Stark daughters she is searching for.

Podrick Payne and the Hound know each other from the time they were both in King's Landing. While Podrick served as the squire for Tyrion Lannister, Sandor Clegane was a member of King Joffrey's Kingsguard, even though he always rejected the appointment to knighthood.

Despite Brienne's statement that she swore an oath to Catelyn Stark to bring her daughters to safety, Sandor, who is named the Hound due to his wild temperament, doubts her real intentions when he recognizes her sword decorated with Lannister gold. Instead, he suspects that she is in their service and they have placed a bounty on his head.

During the Battle of the Blackwater, the "Wildfire", a highly flammable substance which was used there and is normally produced as an incendiary for use in war as it is very difficult to extinguish, reminded the Hound of an early childhood trauma. He then abandoned his own men and fled the capital. Tywin Lannister, again acting as Hand of the King, then placed a bounty of 100 silver stags on his head for his capture.

Encouraged by the Hound's testimony, the initial powerful impression that Brienne seemed to have made on the girl, now visibly disappears. Arya is now also skeptical about Brienne's mission and decides to stay with her companion.

Brienne senses that she may lose Arya and thus she will not be able to keep her oath. With her overpowering voice and insisting on her sworn oath, she desperately tries to convince the girl to come with her.

However, past experience has taught Arya that she should always be cautious of any person, no matter how friendly they seem.

The sword alone, which the Hound mentioned was decorated with Lannister gold, is reason enough for Arya to distrust the woman since they are mainly to blame for the destruction of her family.

Brienne also does not deny her connection to Jaime Lannister, and thus it is clear to Arya that she wants nothing to do with this woman.

But Brienne doubts that the Hound is really protecting the girl like he says he is. And he in turn has no interest in leaving Arya with Brienne whom he thinks is a totally unsuitable woman ("Safety? Where the fuck's that? Her aunt in the Eyrie is dead! Her mother's dead! Her father's dead! Her brother's dead! Winterfell is a pile of rubble! There's no safety, you dumb bitch! If you don't know that by now, you're the wrong one to watch over her!").

Sansa's escape from King's Landing was planned in advance by Petyr Baelish. Dontos Hollard, a former knight, who was made a fool by Joffrey, received the order from Littlefinger to bring Sansa to him on his awaiting ship in the Blackwater Bay immediately after the King's murder. In order to avoid any troublesome witnesses, Baelish had Hollard disposed of. He then went with Sansa to the Eyrie to her aunt Lysa Arryn. Baelish married Catelyn Stark's sister shortly after his arrival, not out of love but to gain a legitimate claim to the Vale of Arryn. Shortly thereafter he murdered her.

Theon Greyjoy, a ward to the Starks due to his father Balon's failed rebellion, betrayed Robb Stark in the War of the Five Kings. Instead of supporting him with the promised fleet of "Ironborn" from his father, Theon turned against the King in the North and took the almost deserted Winterfell with his men to regain the favor of his own father, on the on hand, and to take revenge for being taken as a ward, on the other.
As a result, Robb Stark besieged Winterfell and let it be recaptured by the Boltons. But before the Ironborn handed over the traitor, Theon Greyjoy, to the Boltons in return for safe passage, they almost completely burned down the castle. Winterfell has been in ruins ever since.

Nevertheless, neither Brienne nor the Hound are willing to give in to the other. Both consider themselves the better protector of the Stark girl, ultimately resulting in a bitter duel between the two warriors not at all wanted by the woman.

Since the Hound rejects Brienne's expressed willingness to end the duel in a peaceful manner ("I have no wish to kill you, Ser.") when she manages to temporarily disarm her opponent, she must push herself to her limit and beyond.

Underscored by the menacing-sounding opening bars of Ramin Djawadi's "Oathkeeper", which can already be heard during the verbal altercation between Brienne and the Hound and which then turn into a thumping staccato at the beginning of the duel, the viewer is presented with a truly extraordinary, absolutely evenly matched and excessively dirty fight between man and woman. Brienne must meet uncountable physical demands, and she takes headbutts as well as kicks to the abdomen. But she also knows how to defend herself.

One of the strangest moments of this fight must be when she bites off the Hound's ear and then spits it out. The duel finally comes to an end when Brienne furiously and mercilessly bashes the Hound's face again and again with a fist-sized stone and immense force, and he rolls down a hill.

The entire scene up to the final battle is a wonderful example of how the woman dogmatically sticks to her principles and how she disregards rational considerations.

Despite what the Hound says about protecting Arya and the girl's decision to stay with him, which should have been confirmation enough for the truthfulness of his words, Brienne does not believe him and she probably perceives him as bad company for the Stark girl due to his scruffy appearance and his crude nature.

For me, there are two fundamental reasons why the situation then escalates, eventually leading to a conflict of life and death: stubbornness on both sides in the form of a lack of willingness to cooperate and mutual distrust. If the two squabblers had approached each other and neither had wanted to impose their own strong will, Arya Stark would have actually had the perfect duo of protectors with Brienne and the Hound. Both are extraordinary fighters, and it is hard to imagine more protection than that. The two worlds are only split by their characters.

While Brienne is loyal, dutiful, completely focused on fulfilling her oath and also does not pursue financial interests, the Hound only intends to protect the girl until he can deliver her somewhere safely and, above all, make a profit.

However, both have ultimately lost: the Hound lost the duel against Brienne and she lost track of Arya who has suddenly disappeared.

Despite her exhaustion, though, Brienne still has enough strength to lay into Podrick for letting Arya escape.

The boy really does not have it easy and he would probably have known many places that he would rather be than with her at that moment...

rya was able to use the duel between Brienne and the Hound to hide at some distance from Podrick without being seen.

At the end of the battle and knowing that she escaped Brienne and her squire, the girl creeps towards the severely injured Sandor Clegane lying on the hillside.

Parallels can be drawn between what the Hound says when Arya eventually crouches in front of him and the conversation between Renly Baratheon and Loras Tyrell after Brienne defeated the latter at the tournament at Bitterbridge (Episode 2.03 *What is Dead May Never Die*).

Just like Loras at that time, the Hound is also equally frustrated by losing to Brienne, and thus losing to a woman ("Big bitch saved you. (…) Killed by a woman. I bet you like that."). However, the only difference to the earlier scene is that the Knight of the Flowers escaped with just a few minor injuries. Whereas things are not looking so good for the Hound...

In this case, the slightly disrespectful expression relating to Brienne's appearance is probably not meant personally, but, like Loras at that time, it functions as verbal protection to vent his irritation at being defeated by a woman. If someone is sending him into the great beyond, then please make it a man! However, even if the term "bitch" was somehow understandable from his point of view, the Hound who once ruthlessly assaulted peaceful farmers with his distinct mercenary mentality is certainly not a sympathetic figure either.

However, Arya rejects the Hound's subsequent advice for her to join Brienne because after all that she has learned about her so far, she cannot and does not wish to trust the tall blonde woman.

When he eventually begs Arya to release him from his suffering and to kill him, it becomes clear how much she has been influenced by the long time spent travelling with him. This time has made the Stark girl just as merciless and tough as the Hound was to others. He is now becoming the victim of what he did to her. Rather than fulfilling his final wish and thus striking him off her list of all those who have caused suffering to herself, her family or people who were close to her, Arya takes the dying man's moneybag and leaves him to his fate.

Dead men, he once told her, don't need silver...

A Review of Season Four

This season is just as strong as the previous season but it has a completely different focus.

While she was just a punching bag for other characters and often suffered their humiliations in season three, we get to see another Brienne here: a warrior who must more or less plan her next steps by herself.

The fact that life at court is seemingly not for the Lady of Tarth is not really surprising now, since she has always rejected it. What is new, however, is that Brienne reveals one of her (admittedly few) negative sides to the viewer for the first time in this season when she receives a squire, Podrick Payne, who she considers incompetent and useless from the outset and therefore treats him rather shabbily.

For me, this season has two truly outstanding moments. Firstly, the renewed farewell scene between Brienne and Jaime (Episode 4.04 *Oathkeeper*) when he equips her with new armor and gives her a valuable sword made of Valyrian steel as a sign of his appreciation before sending her on a mission to find Sansa Stark (now Lannister) and bring her to safety. The underlying tension between these two characters from season three is also clearly noticeable here.

The second outstanding moment is obviously the gripping and action-packed duel between Brienne and the Hound in the course of her encounter with Arya Stark in the final episode. I was already quite aware that Brienne knows how to handle a sword extremely well, but the fact that she can confront the Hound, one of the most feared and hot-tempered warriors of Westeros, in the same merciless and brutal way that he faces her, and ultimately defeat him due to her enormous physique, was a really big deal.

Season Five

The Wars to Come

> **Location:**
> **around 10 miles west of the "Bloody Gate", Vale of Arryn**

Losing Arya in the end despite her efforts is a personal defeat for Brienne and she has literally given up. Fortunately, she has someone to vent to in such cases, namely Podrick...

While the boy is in the process of planning their next steps during a rest break since, after the loss of Arya, they can now devote their attention to finding Arya's sister, Sansa, Brienne sees no reason at all to continue dragging her unwanted companion along and, furthermore, out of danger ("The only reason you're here is because Jaime Lannister told me you weren't safe in the capital. You're hundreds of miles from King's Landing. No one knows what you look like. No one cares. You're safe.").

In addition to Podrick's rudimentary riding skills, his virtually non-existent culinary skills and his demonstrated inability to tether horses so that they do not run away, he also let Arya slip away. What should Brienne do with someone who fails at such simple tasks?

"I don't want anyone following me. I'm not a leader. All I ever wanted was to fight for a lord I believed in. The good lords are dead and the rest are monsters."
- **Brienne to Podrick Payne**

However, Podrick sees no alternative to remaining with her and consequently makes no effort to leave her. He is now her squire.

And since Brienne's lack of motivation has obviously not escaped his notice as such, he tries to encourage the deeply shaken Maiden of Tarth to continue the search with reference to her oath, regardless of her new attempt to get rid of him.

On the other hand, Brienne is increasingly realizing that her self-chosen ideal of serving a good lord appears to be an almost hopeless endeavour. If she were to try to chase and catch her own shadow, she would probably have a much greater chance of success...

If it was Brienne who tried to lift Jaime up morally after his mutilation (Episode 3.04 *And Now His Watch is Ended*), it is now Podrick who, albeit a little hesitantly, tries to dissuade his companion, who is stoically occupied the whole time to cultivate and sharpen her sword, from giving up. However, he only has moderate success. The frustration about her failure that now blasts Podrick in the face like a sharp wind all the time ("Will you shut your mouth? I didn't ask for your advice!"), is too much.

Of course, in the overall picture of this chain of unfortunate circumstances, it fits in nicely that Podrick sees a carriage being escorted by several riders of the Vale passing not far from the two during their small disagreement, without knowing that in this moment they are closer to their objective than ever before. An almost absurd scene...

Very keen observers of the scene may have noticed that our duo is now in possession of a horse again (can be seen immediately at the beginning of the sequence before it disappears from the screen due to the camera movement to the left). Let us recall: the two have been travelling by foot for many miles thanks to the boy's active "efforts".

But it is unclear where the horse came from. It is likely that Brienne took the Hound's horse after their duel and Arya left on her own horse when she abandoned the Hound to fend for himself. It is also possible that Brienne managed to recover at least one of their lost animals in the meantime. It presumably did not fall from the sky...

Whatever the combination may be: one horse for two people meant that Podrick was the loser of the popular children's game "musical chairs" in any case.

The House of Black and White

Location:
initially at an inn near the East Road, later in the surrounding woods, Vale of Arryn

While on their path, which is seemingly aimless at present, Brienne and Podrick stop for a bite to eat at an inn in the Vale of Arryn.

Just the manner in which the two head for the inn reminds me a little of two other literary figures: Miguel de Cervantes' "Don Quixote" and his loyal servant "Sancho Panza", only with the difference that Brienne here plays the female "Knight of Sad Countenance" and Podrick is not riding a donkey but he is walking beside her in the absence of a second horse.

While Brienne picks at her food in a demoralized and listless way and muses to herself, Podrick identifies Sansa, who Brienne is searching for, on one of the neighboring tables accompanied by Petyr "Littlefinger" Baelish and several knights of House Arryn. From his time as Tyrion's squire Tyrions's wife is, of course, no stranger to him.

Following Lysa Arryn's murder, who he had quickly married shortly before, Littlefinger is with his niece-in-law, Sansa, on the way from the Eyrie heading west, escorted by an entourage of knights of the Vale of Arryn. Destination: unknown.

With this news, Podrick manages to suddenly light up Brienne's face with a glimmer of hope and excitement. Perhaps this is her positive twist of fate after the recent setback! Despite Podrick's warning to hold back and be cautious, Brienne goes to Littlefinger's table, but not before sending her companion out to find enough horses just in case.

This scene is a good example of how rash and stubborn Brienne can sometimes be. Since, in contrast to the previous situation when she did not want to leave the dead Renly's side (Episode 2.05 *The Ghost of Harrenhal*) or when the conflict with the Hound ultimately culminated in an avoidable duel (Episode 4.10 *The Children*), knight's honor and ethical conduct play no role here, in my opinion.

Instead of initially keeping a low profile, monitoring the situation from afar and then carefully planning their next steps, Brienne goes straight over to Littlefinger even though she became acquainted with Petyr Baelish and his deviousness during the meeting at Renly Baratheon's camp (Episode 2.04 *Garden of Bones*) and he can be seen with several knights for his protection.

Perhaps the reason for her action in this situation is less "even though" and more "because" she knows Littlefinger. Perhaps she is building on precisely the fact that she and the man from the Fingers had already met in Renly's camp and the latter praised her loyalty and discretion beyond all measure in Baelish's presence (Episode 2.04 *Garden of Bones*). Perhaps she therefore thinks that the situation is completely harmless and that nothing would stand in her way if she asks Sansa to come with her.

However, the only catch is that Brienne does not have much time for political entanglements and alliances. She is unaware that Baelish was actually behind Joffrey's murder. She is unaware that he pushed Sansa's aunt Lysa to her death. But, above all, she is unaware of what role the girl has to play in Littlefinger's considerations and why she is now with him. With this in mind, she would have certainly acted differently... Thus, she remains uncritical at first.

Petyr Baelish also remembers their encounter at Renly Baratheon's camp at Storm's End well, as along with the fact that she was part of that meeting as a member of his Kingsguard. However, he immediately destroys Brienne's hopes for a light-hearted conversation when he ruthlessly suggests that her loyalty, which was once so highly praised by Renly as free of charge, now appears to have given way to opportunistic thoughts ("We've met with Renly Baratheon. What did he say about you? He said your loyalty came free of charge. Someone appears to have paid quite a lot since then.") in his typical, cynical manner after noticing her new armor and the gold-decorated sword.

With this statement, Littlefinger accuses Brienne of precisely his own behavior and mentality when he eventually asks her to come to his table. What a sly dog!

Brienne can certainly be accused of a few things but least of all unscrupulousness. Perhaps she would have embarked on the search for Sansa with a nightgown and cake fork if she had not received the sword and armor from Jaime Lannister. Based on her facial expression, she appears to resent Baelish for his statement.

Without wasting any time, Brienne now offers her sword to Sansa with reference to her sworn oath to protect her, like she did her sister Arya, who refused. In my opinion, Brienne kneeling before the Stark girl is reminiscent of her pledge of allegiance to Sansa's mother Catelyn in *The Ghost of Harrenhal* (Episode 2.05) and it is just as solemn.

"Lady Sansa, before your mother's death, I was her sworn sword. I gave my word I would find you and protect you. I will shield your back and keep your counsel and give my life for yours if need be. I swear it by the Old Gods and the New." - **Brienne to Sansa Lannister**

However, Littlefinger has no intention of entrusting the girl to an outsider like Brienne and he reveals her failures with regard to Renly Baratheon and Catelyn Stark to Sansa, thus the people to whom she had offered her protection ("This woman swore to protect Renly. She failed. She swore to protect your mother. She failed. Why would I want somebody with your history of failure guarding Lady Sansa?").

Yet it is apparently not only Littlefinger's plausible-sounding and manipulatively chosen words that are reason enough for Sansa to reject Brienne's protection. She also accuses the woman of having bowed before Joffrey at his wedding ceremony and thus showing her subservience to him. But is Sansa's rejection of Brienne really full of conviction? Or is she just following the same line as Baelish to prevent her guardian from knowing her real intentions? It is impossible to tell from this scene.

In any case, I think that her rejection of Brienne's help was the best thing Sansa could have done in this situation, both for herself and our protagonist.

At the latest Littlefinger's admission to her that he was one of the puppet masters behind Joffrey's murder (Episode 4.03 *Breaker of Chains*) and the fact that she witnessed him dispose of her aunt Lysa in the most uncharming way with her own eyes, make it clear to Sansa that the man is pursuing a clear objective and that she is an important, if not the most important, pawn in his game.

He would never have simply allowed her to go with Brienne. And since the Maiden of Tarth could be her only salvation and the only trump card she has to escape from Baelish's dubious power games, it would possibly be tactically unwise to jeopardize this advantage without acute need (so far). Therefore, in my opinion, Sansa's subsequent request for Brienne to leave could also be understood as "I do not know who you are, and I do not know whether I can trust you. But if you value your life, make sure you disappear from here!"

Since Brienne now knows Sansa's whereabouts, though, and Baelish must fear that the tall woman could intentionally or thoughtlessly divulge this information, he dubiously asks her to stay and enjoy the protection of the knights accompanying him.

From this moment on, it is completely irrelevant as to whether Sansa's request to Brienne really was a hidden indication to make her escape as quickly as possible and as to whether the woman registered it as such. Brienne's suspicious look alone shows that she senses a trap in this friendly suggestion, to keep an eye on her, or even to kill her as a troublesome witness.

She eventually, hastily takes flight from the tavern and kills one of the pursuing knights of the Vale in the process. Shortly thereafter, during the subsequent ride through the woods, Podrick, who has been able to organize a second horse, and Brienne become involuntarily separated when the boy's horse suddenly gallops in a different direction.

The woman is able to trick and shake off her pursuers but Podrick is nearby in great danger as two knights of the Vale of Arryn are chasing him. By following the noises and loud neighing of horses, Brienne manages to find her companion in dire need and she makes short work of the two knights.

The chase through the woods of the Vale of Arryn is Brienne's first action sequence on horseback and it is rapidly paced and excitingly staged. On the contrary, Podrick's further plot once again provides the comedy element after his grill fiasco in Episode 4.05 (*First of His Name*) when he is thrown off his horse and lands in a river after trying to bring his horse under control.

Brienne comes to Podrick's rescue in the end. A scene which is highly interesting in two respects. On the one hand, because the viewer sees the difference between Valyrian and conventional steel for the first time when she effortlessly shatters her second opponent's sword with

Oathkeeper, and on the other, because we learn that she is not indifferent to what happens to Podrick, despite her dislike towards him.

After everything that has happened, one could assume that his doom would be convenient for her since there will probably never be a better opportunity for her to rid herself of him. The fact alone that she is not thinking this way clearly speaks for Brienne's thoroughly noble character. Following her knights code, she does not have the heart to abandon a person entrusted to her, no matter her relationship to him.

Although Podrick now considers Brienne's oath to be expired, unlike during their previous rest break since both Stark daughters refused her help ("My lady, if both Stark girls refused your service, maybe you're released from your vow."), Brienne sees that the girl is in great danger with Littlefinger and she decides to follow him and Sansa...

High Sparrow

Location:
near Moat Cailin, the North

A s previously mentioned, Brienne and Podrick secretly follow Baelish's escort party. From a safe distance and the protection of a hill, the two observe how the entourage on the Kingsroad approach Moat Cailin, a partly destroyed stronghold in the swampy border region between the North and the Riverlands. Since Brienne believes to know where Littlefinger is heading, she can afford to take a detour around the castle and refrains from staying close on his heels.

During a subsequent rest break and when Brienne asks how he actually came into the service of Tyrion Lannister, Podrick willingly divulges. He was almost hanged together with his previous lord due to a careless misdemeanor by the latter. His neck was ultimately only saved because of his family name "Payne".

Podrick Payne is a distant relative of the royal executioner Ser Ilyn Payne. He was eventually pardoned by Tywin Lannister because of this family relationship and sent to squire for his son, Tyrion.

When, at the end of his statement, Podrick adds that Tyrion always treated him well, Brienne knows, of course, that this cannot be said of her. Realizing this fact, she replies with an almost self-pitying "Yes, all your lords have been very kind to you. All except me.".

However, instead of agreeing with her, Podrick highly praises her impressive sword skills and adds that he counts himself lucky to serve as her squire ("You're the best fighter I've ever seen. You beat the Hound. I'm proud to be your squire.").

A statement that should permanently change the relationship between the two for the better...

It is not only because these are probably the most beautiful and honest words that she has heard for a long time since the viewer has the feeling that the Lady of Tarth must hold back so as not to burst into tears. No, the fact that these words are also coming from someone who she constantly snapped at and patronized from the beginning was certainly not only a complete surprise to her but also to any observer.

Brienne knows that her behavior towards him was not always right and sometimes even mean. The fact that she eventually apologizes to Podrick for this manner ("I'm sorry I'm always snapping at you.") indicates true greatness. Not everybody would be willing to admit their mistakes so openly.

Her subsequent offer (perhaps of reparation) to train him in sword fighting and horseback riding, which Podrick jubilantly accepts, also reveals that she is now finally prepared to put her absolute trust in him and "take a leap of faith".

An impression that intensifies in the following scene when Brienne also reveals her past in reply to Podrick's question while allowing him to help her out of her armor without objection. It was not so very long ago (Episode 4.05 *First of His Name*) that she had rigorously rejected his assistance.

"'Brienne the Beauty' they called me. Great joke. And I realized I was the ugliest girl alive. A great lumbering beast!" - **Brienne to Podrick Payne**

She reveals her innermost secrets when she confesses to him how her father wanted to provide her with an appropriate husband when she was a young girl, but she was secretly ridiculed by all the eligible young lords because of her appearance and it was only Renly Baratheon who consoled her and thus saved her from "being a joke". Since that day and despite her knowledge of his inclination for men, she revered the youngest of the three Baratheon brothers and even felt something like love for him.

"Nothing's more hateful than failing to protect the one you love. One day I will avenge Renly. (…) I know it was Stannis. I know it in my heart. Stannis is a man, not a shadow. And a man can be killed." - **Brienne to Podrick Payne**

This open-heartedness finally unravels Brienne's relationship to Renly and answers the question as to why she was so profoundly shocked after his murder. He had saved her from becoming a laughing stock in her childhood. But by contrast, she could not do anything for him. Even worse: she had to watch as he died in her arms. This pain is still deeply rooted. She still blames herself for this failure. Her desire to take revenge on Stannis Baratheon for the treacherous and cowardly murder of his younger brother and her King is now even greater.

Brienne's change of mood during her story is remarkable here. We see how the events of that time still affect her emotionally. Her initially happy, yet melancholic expression visibly fills with bitterness through her disappointment and corresponding thirst for revenge more or less simultaneously with the described events. The quiet and seemingly menacing version of Djawadi's "The Old Gods and the New" provides the absolutely harmonious background music.

Certainly, Brienne is not the sort of person who simply proclaims such intimate details because she feels like it, quite apart from the fact that she is not one of the more loquacious characters in the story. Nevertheless, she willingly and elaborately reveals a traumatic experience from her past to Podrick.

Indeed, it seems that she now sees the boy as more than just a good listener and as someone to be trusted, a reliable and genuine (although sometimes clumsy) companion.

Even though I consider Brienne's action scenes as truly magnificent, like the duel with the Hound or her daring escape on horseback through the woods of the Vale of Arryn, I realized from this scene that my favorite sequences are actually her calm and emotional ones, like her pledge of allegiance to Catelyn Stark, the various farewell scenes with Jaime or now this profound conversation with Podrick.

And this was certainly not the last of these sequences...

Sons of the Harpy

Location:
Narrow Sea east of the Isle of Tarth, Stormlands

In his role as Hand of the King and against the will of his sister Cersei, Tyrion Lannister had her daughter, Myrcella, shipped away to Dorne before the imminent Battle of the Blackwater for safety reasons and to ensure an allegiance between the two houses Martell and Baratheon, affirmed by a planned wedding between Trystan Martell and the Baratheon daughter.

After Tyrion was much later arrested as the suspected murderer of King Joffrey, he insisted on judgement by the Gods at the subsequent trial in the form of a judicial duel and put his fate in the hands of Oberyn Martell, the Prince of Dorne. However, Oberyn was brutally killed and Tyrion was sentenced to death.

Fearing that Oberyn's older brother, Prince Doran, could now retaliate for the death of his brother, Cersei gave her brother Jaime the order to travel to Dorne and bring back Princess Myrcella who was now in acute danger.

Since an army would attract too much attention, Jaime sets out with his only companion Bronn, a former mercenary and Tyrion's bodyguard until his arrest, on a neutral merchant ship to the southernmost region of the Seven Kingdoms.

When the ship passes an island on the way to Dorne and the Captain answers Jaime's question as to whether it is Estermont in the negative ("Tarth, Ser Jaime. The Sapphire Isle"), his sparkling eyes indicate that just the sound of the name "Tarth" alone brings back fond memories for him.

Memories of a woman who he initially found repulsive and who he savagely demeaned but for who he ultimately developed friendly feelings and even affection and who he does not know whether he will ever see her again...

It is a short sequence lasting only a few seconds, and it may have passed by viewers who follow this storyline without paying particular attention. However, I bet this scene could not be short enough for someone who cares about Brienne and misses her.

Sometimes looks say more than words...

Incidentally, this scene is accompanied again by the well-established "The Old Gods and the New", even though Brienne does not appear in person here but only in Jaime's thoughts.

Episode 5.05
Kill the Boy

Location:
Inn in Winter Town near Winterfell, the North

Brienne's suspicions were right. Littlefinger's destination was in fact Winterfell, but the former family seat of the Starks, and thus Sansa's home, has been under the control of the Boltons for some time.

Since Winterfell was an abandoned ruin for a long time, it now serves as the seat of House Bolton, the new "Wardens of the North", and is in the process of restoration.

In order to remain undetected, Brienne and Podrick find accommodation at an inn in the nearby Winter Town.

The fact that going together in one direction does not necessarily mean always holding the same view is demonstrated in relation to the question as to whether Sansa is now safe with the Boltons or not.

While the boy believes that Sansa is probably safe from the Lannisters in Winterfell, a contemplative Brienne can in no way agree with this view. She still considers the Stark girl to be in extreme danger. After all, she is now in the hands of those to whom half of her family fell victim at the Twins ("Better off with the Boltons, who murdered her mother and brother?").

"I served Lady Catelyn. I serve her still. Who do you serve?" - **Brienne to inn servant**

Brienne recognizes in an old inn servant, who randomly comes into her chamber to bring fresh water, that there is clearly still enough sympathy and loyalty for the almost eradicated Starks in the North and she asks him to get a message to Sansa.

Although the old man is initially suspicious about why the tall woman needs his help, he then seems extremely impressed by her determination to help the Stark daughter.

Of course, Brienne's attempt to ask the stranger for help poses a certain risk because there is ultimately no guarantee that he really is one of the few Stark loyalists and not a spy for the Boltons. But perhaps Brienne was convinced that she could trust him by his anxious and almost wistful expression when mentioning the name "Stark" and the fact that he seems to be just as skeptical as her. And furthermore: what is it they say? Nothing ventured, nothing gained...

Have I forgotten to mention something? Oh, yes! Djawadi's "The Old Gods and the New" can also be heard quietly in the background as usual.

Brienne was not mistaken about the old man. Her message actually reaches Sansa inside the castle through a worker who is clearly still loyal to the Starks ("You still have friends in the North. (…) You're not alone.").

She anonymously offers her help to the eldest Stark daughter in this message. Should Sansa ever be in danger, she should light a candle in the highest window of the "Broken Tower" as a sign.

The Gift

> **Location:**
> **outside Winterfell, the North**

Brienne patiently watches the window of the Broken Tower from a safe distance while snow begins to fall, so that she can take action in the event that Sansa actually gives the agreed signal.

However, the woman knows nothing about the dramatic turn of events taking place within the castle walls of Winterfell...

I think it makes sense at this point to take a brief look into the heart of the action und the characters involved – in Winterfell:

Even though Sansa Stark was married to Tyrion Lannister for some time, this marriage was never really valid according to the customs of the Seven Kingdoms since it was never consummated. Petyr "Littlefinger" Baelish, Sansa's uncle-in-law, subsequently set out with his niece from the Eyrie to Winterfell. He saw the opportunity to take the North bit by bit by having Sansa marry Roose Bolton's bastard son and heir, Ramsay. However, Ramsay is anything but a caring husband. He is cruel, unscrupulous and presumably what is commonly referred to as a sadistic psychopath. After weeks of psychological and physical torture, which eventually culminated in her rape on their wedding night, the girl takes the decision to escape from her ordeal with the help of Theon Greyjoy, the former Stark ward...

Once the Boltons could recapture Winterfell, which was occupied by the Ironborn, they allowed the islanders to leave, but the traitor Theon Greyjoy was to be surrendered to Robb Stark. However, contrary to what was planned, the heir of the Iron Islands was taken to an unknown location in the North by his captors. There Theon was tortured by Ramsay, who cut off his manhood and made him his submissive pet with the degrading name "Reek". Sansa now sees her last glimmer of hope for help escaping Winterfell in Theon, who spent his childhood with the eldest Stark daughter, among others, due to his time as a ward, and she asks him to place a burning candle in the Broken Tower.
Theon declares himself willing but being thoroughly frightened and the physical and psychological wreck that he is after Ramsay's torture, he takes the proverbial "left turn" at the aforementioned tower and quickly tells his lord about Sansa's escape plan.

Episode 5.10
Mother's Mercy

While Brienne is still tirelessly watching the window of the Broken Tower, not far away Podrick spots Stannis Baratheon from a forest clearing completely unexpectedly marching on Winterfell with the rest of his army.

After he was led to the wall by Melisandre's prophecy that the real war would not take place in the South but in the North, Stannis and his army managed to save the Night's Watch from the numerically superior Wildings at Castle Black in the nick of time. He and his men stayed there to prepare his next step – to free the North from the hands of the Boltons.

Even though there is hardly a leader in the Seven Kingdoms who can match him in terms of warfare, Stannis made the mistake of relying too much on Melisandre's prophecies. Thus, Stannis, who is completely convinced of the power of the Red God, even sacrificed his own daughter Shireen, when he and his men were caught off guard by the sudden onset of winter and faced starvation on the way to Winterfell. Half of his army deserted him and took all the horses. Still driven by ambition, he was forced to carry out his assault on Winterfell with the pitiful rest of his army on foot. A hopeless endeavor...

The boy immediately rushes to Brienne and gives her the news. She is torn between on the one hand, the opportunity to now finally be able to take revenge on Stannis for Renly's murder and, on the other, the want to keep her oath to bring the Stark girl to safety. When she eventually decides to take revenge on Stannis and turns her back to the window in the Broken Tower, sure enough, the candle is lit...

This somehow fits the tragedy of the character of "Brienne" and the fact that fate has conspired against her. Once again, she is so close to her goal that she loses it. And it cannot be said that she is always to blame for this. How can a single person be so unlucky? She watches the aforementioned window in the Broken Tower day in, day out for weeks in the hope of seeing Sansa's signal there in the near future, and nothing happens. If only Podrick had not suddenly come running to tell her that Stannis Baratheon was within her reach, she would have kept her eye on the window and not missed the agreed sign.

With one last, desperate look to the window, her tension can be felt, as well as her dilemma that she will inevitably have to put one of her two oaths on hold. A decision that is clearly difficult for her to take.

The parallels here to the scene when Jaime Lannister tried to persuade her to kill the farmer (Episode 3.02 *Dark*

Wings, Dark Words) and she faced the difficult decision of what she should do, are unmistakable. Her morality triumphed back then.

Of course, it was not expected that Stannis Baratheon would suddenly appear here and now from her point of view. The reason that she then ultimately brings herself to leave her post to take revenge for Renly's murder could be linked to the fact that she very quickly considered which of these two objectives would be more achievable in the very near future.

Yet, although Stannis is in close proximity, it is absolutely possible that he could be killed by one of the Boltons due to the impending battle and thus she would be deprived of her revenge. Speed is therefore of the essence.

Then again, since she had waited for weeks in vain for Sansa's signal, the probability that the agreed sign would be sent now of all times is almost zero. If she mindlessly continues to watch the window, she runs the risk of eventually coming away completely empty-handed with regards to the fulfilment of her oaths.

Nevertheless, I am completely certain of one thing: if she would have seen the candle signal at the same moment when Podrick gave her the news of Stannis' appearance and thus she would have had the choice to either take revenge on Stannis or to rescue Sansa, she would have opted for the Stark girl. Brienne's previous way of thinking and acting ultimately leads to no other conclusion. She would certainly have put the protection of the Stark daughter over her own desire for revenge.

An assessment shared by Gwendoline Christie herself, who appeared as a guest on the British talk show *Thronecast* on Sky Atlantic after the broadcast of the tenth and final episode, and who gave the following answer when host Sue Perkins asked for her opinion on which of the two options Brienne would have chosen:

"I'd like to think, she would have gone to Sansa".

Location:
Wolfswood, east of Winterfell, The North

*A*fter a costly battle for Winterfell, which was ultimately lost due to numerical inferiority, Brienne finds the seriously injured and grief-stricken Stannis Baratheon leaning against a tree.

Finally, it seems the day of reckoning has come for her. She now has the opportunity to take revenge and she confronts Stannis about the murder of his brother Renly.

When he confesses his direct involvement, Brienne sentences him to death. She draws her sword and swings it in his direction...

Did she do it or not? Since the scene ended and cut off at the actual moment the sword strikes as a so-called "cliffhanger" for dramatic reasons, some doubts remain as to whether Brienne really killed Stannis and whether he finally got his just desserts for all his misjudgements which also cost the life of his daughter Shireen, among others.

Indeed, over the years, *Game of Thrones* has repeatedly taught us that we should only believe it when we see it, and Stannis' death was withheld from the viewer. However, in contrast to the scene at the end of season four when Arya leaves the Hound dying, it is not hard to believe that Stannis actually met his maker here. Oathkeeper came down on him too powerfully and clearly. Unfortunately. Not that I feel strongly about the character of Stannis Baratheon. He ultimately had his own brother assassinated, needlessly sacrificed his daughter and thus drove his wife Selyse to suicide. This does not necessarily make him a sympathetic figure for me. Though it is not Brienne's style to simply execute a defenseless and injured person, no matter what he did previously.

Perhaps she was expecting a duel, man versus woman, the same eye level (okay, this seems rather difficult considering her size, but it is meant only as a figure of speech).

There is something anticlimactic about the fact that she now sees him leaning helpless and exhausted against a tree, thus making it incomparably easier for her to take revenge. It is precisely this act of execution that leaves her looking a little like a cold-blooded monster. She has an extremely strong desire for revenge but this is also absolutely under-standable...

"In the name of Renly of House Baratheon, First of His name, rightful King of the Andals and the First Men, Lord of the Seven Kingdoms and Protector of the Realm. I, Brienne of Tarth, sentence you to die."
- **Brienne to Stannis Baratheon**

When the avenging angel is suddenly standing in front of him in the form of Brienne, one could have expected Stannis to make one last act of defiance by shouting "Renly was gay but he was no king!" or something similar before she enforced her judgement. Instead, when she asks if he has any last words, he simply brings himself to say, "Go on, do your duty", in surrender. He is aware that his journey has now come to an end. And he also appears to accept his fate according to his desperate facial expression. He has noth-ing left worth living for. He ultimately has his entire family on his conscience and he led his army to disaster.

A Review of Season Five

This season consisted of two things: waiting and – what was the second again? Oh, yes, waiting....
A development of her plot line that was certainly not to be expected when considering Brienne's action-packed start to this season.

Nevertheless, these low-stress, slowed-down scenes also have a certain significance: they once again underline Brienne's stubbornness, that giving up is not an option for her (even if she was on the verge at one point) and her determined will to keep her once sworn oath.

In particular, three scenes from this season remained with me.
The first scene is the previously mentioned first class and excitingly staged chase on horseback through the woods in the Vale of Arryn when Brienne must escape from the knights of the Vale and her riding skills are finally put to use.
The second scene is simultaneously one of my absolute favorite scenes from the entire Brienne plot when she reveals herself to Podrick and confesses her fateful and truly stirring life story to him. A completely new facet of Brienne can be seen here as she allows someone to look into her mental abyss. At the same time, it is a sequence that shows that the Maiden of Tarth also has sufficient self-reflection to reconsider and change her behavior.
Finally, the third scene the execution of the man who she primarily blames for Renly's murder: Stannis Baratheon.
After weeks of perseverance and tirelessly waiting for a candle signal, which, to lend the necessary tragedy to her efforts, of course, only appears when she has left her observation post, she fulfils her oath to avenge her former

lord's murder. Even if the manner of enforcement is somewhat bloodthirsty.

However, I call it straightforward. Firm but fair. Just as one
might expect from her.

Season Six

Episode 6.01
The Red Woman

Meanwhile, the news that Stannis Baratheon was killed during the battle for Winterfell has spread behind the castle walls.

Though when Roose Bolton's now-legitimized bastard son Ramsay cannot tell his father who was ultimately responsible for the death of "the false king", the new Warden of the North finds this very unfortunate since he would reward the man who killed Stannis. Nevertheless, he considers it a great victory over the Baratheon army.

The fact that Stannis was not killed by a man but by a woman would probably be of secondary importance for Roose Bolton, should he ever become aware of it. Likewise, he would disregard Brienne's actual reason for it. She was not concerned about the defense of Winterfell. She was driven purely and simply by taking revenge for Renly's murder. Consequently, Stannis' death is what would now be described as a win-win situation for both the Boltons and the woman.

If, after the end of the fifth season, there was still a small question mark as to whether Stannis was actually killed by Brienne's sword stroke or not, then this conversation between father and son at the beginning of the sixth season allays any last doubts early on.

Location:
Wolfswood, east of Winterfell, the North

Sansa was able to use the general confusion caused by the attack on Winterfell by Stannis Baratheon's troops and escape from her chamber where her husband Ramsay had kept her captive for a long time. She made her way to the Broken Tower and lit the candle as agreed. But the promised help did not come because Brienne had to leave her observation post with the intention of taking revenge on Stannis.

Without any prospect of rescue by the stranger(s) from outside, Sansa then attempted to escape Winterfell with the help of Theon Greyjoy/Reek, who had come back to his senses, by jumping together from the castle wall to the ground and, hopefully, to freedom...

Having survived their daring leap from the Winterfell castle wall, Sansa and Theon are now fleeing through the snowy Wolfswood.

However, since Ramsay does not intend to let his "plaything" and wife Sansa, who should ultimately provide him with an heir to secure the North for his House, get away so easily, he sends half a dozen of his best soldiers after them with tracking dogs to recapture the fugitives.

The Stark girl (now Lady Bolton) and the former Stark ward are quickly caught by their pursuers. But before the Bolton followers can drag the two back to Winterfell, they are surprised and attacked by Brienne and Podrick who ride towards them out of nowhere with drawn swords.

While Brienne's sudden appearance seems quite random at first sight, it is quite likely that she became aware of Sansa and Theon's pursuers due to the loud dog barking, among other things, besides the fact that she was already in Wolfswood with Podrick.

Like before during the duel with the Hound, Brienne must take quite a beating here. She is knocked off her horse and takes a few kicks while lying in the snow right at the beginning of the fight. Nevertheless, she subsequently manages to defeat three of the men in a relatively short time. Brienne was already extremely merciless during the fight scenes in season two (Episodes 2.05 *The Ghost of Harrenhal* and 2.10 *Valar morghulis*) and season four (Episode 4.10 *The Children*). She is no different here, as she frenziedly slits the throats of two of her opponents. The fact that one of these opponents is relatively helpless, pinned down by his own horse, does not appear to be a real mitigating circumstance for her.

As sensitive and vulnerable as she can sometimes be, she is ice cold and uncompromising when it comes to fighting for life and death.

Although Brienne's style of fighting is still impressive, it ultimately provides nothing new for the viewer.

But what, or rather who surprises, is Podrick. The horse riding and fencing training that Brienne promised him during their rest break in the Vale of Arryn (Episode 5.03 *High Sparrow*), is obviously already paying off, because, after all, he succeeds in dispatching one of the Bolton henchmen. However, in the end, he is lucky that Theon appears to be himself again when he stabs another attacker in the back with a sword just before he tries to kill Podrick who is already disarmed and sitting on the seat of his pants.

Incidentally, this scene has excellent, albeit reverse, parallels with the Battle of the Blackwater (Episode 2.09 *Blackwater*). At that time, Podrick saved Lord Tyrion Lannister's life by stabbing Kingsguard Ser Mandon Moor from behind when he tried to kill the defenseless Tyrion. This time, Podrick is saved from death in a similar way.

After the end of the battle, surrounded by lots of red snow and the six lifeless corpses of the Bolton minions, Sansa, who had sought protection under an uprooted tree during the battle, now dares to come out of her hiding place and eventually meets Brienne, the woman whose help she had declined some time ago.

Despite knowing that Sansa had rejected her help at the inn in the Vale of Arryn, Brienne does not remonstrate with her in this respect, but she reverently lays Oathkeeper between herself and the eldest Stark daughter without saying a word.

"Lady Sansa, I offer my services once again. I will shield
your back and keep your counsel and give my life for yours
if need be. I swear it by the Old Gods and the New."
- **Brienne to Sansa Bolton**

When Brienne kneels before the Stark girl and offers her
protection for the second time after their encounter at the
inn, it is a completely new situation for her. While she had
Petyr Baelish by her side at that time, someone who could
do away with any inconveniences and make decisions for
her, she is now responsible for herself.
Uncertain whether she should accept Brienne's offer or
not, she looks at Theon for help. When he eventually sig-
nals that she can trust and take the tall woman into her service with a short nod, Sansa finally follows his unspoken
advice.
She has difficulty reciprocating Brienne's oath of allegiance word-perfectly with the customary sayings, thus she
must briefly turn to Podrick for help with the words "meat
and mead".

During Sansa's reciprocation, something like excited ex-
pectation and hope can be seen in Brienne's eyes. And

apart from the fact that Podrick's swordsmanship is slowly making progress, his knowledge of social customs is always impressive.

Sansa's small faux pas is all too understandable. Until then, it had always been the duty of her deceased parents to receive and make such mutual promises, and now the eldest Stark daughter is suddenly confronted with it and she seems a little helpless and overburdened at this moment.

At the end of her speech, she then nobly asks Brienne to arise. It is such a wonderful moment that burned into my mind in a very short time and of which I can now say, without blushing, that it is my absolute favorite scene. Misty eyes and all.

Ultimately keeping her once sworn oath to Catelyn Stark and thus fulfilling her heart's desire after many months full of setbacks, hardships and dangers is certainly not just incredibly poignant and liberating for the Lady of Tarth. It also brings an end to the long dry spell for the viewer, wondering whether she could ever keep that oath. It is, therefore, not really surprising that this woman, who is otherwise so cool and sometimes unapproachable, lets her feelings (and yes, her tears as well) run free with an expression of relief, pride and inner joy.

One might think that this is the end of the series. All's well that ends well. But, alas, this is *Game of Thrones*, and it is likely that the four will soon be torn away from their momentary comfort zone.

Once again, of course, "The Old Gods and the New" can be heard in this scene. Simply one musical piece for the very special Brienne moments. Perhaps the composer should have simply named it "Brienne's Theme"...

Home

After Lord Rickard Karstark killed two captured Lannister boys as scapegoats in self-administered justice for losing his revenge on the Kingslayer, Robb Stark punished this treason by beheading the leader of the Karstarks. This then broke their oath of allegiance to the Starks so that they joined the Boltons under the leadership of their new Lord, Rickard Karstark's son Harald.

In order to compensate for the losses after the battle against Stannis Baratheon's army and thus to be able to effectively protect Winterfell against enemies, the Karstarks were summoned by Roose Bolton to the former family seat of the Starks.

After arriving at the castle, Harald Karstark, the new leader of the house allied with the Boltons, informs Roose Bolton and his son Ramsay that he encountered the dead bodies of the hunters that should have brought Sansa Bolton and Theon Greyjoy back in the Wolfswood on his way to Winterfell.

In response to Ramsay's assumption that the escapees obviously had help, his father promptly comments by stating that the Stark girl had not "killed them all by herself" in his typical mocking manner.

This assessment by the new Lord of Winterfell is correct. Of course, Sansa had help, and what help it was! Roose Bolton probably would have rewarded Brienne for the execution of Stannis Baratheon, as already mentioned. In contrast, his enthusiasm for the slaughtering of his best hunters would have been limited.

Sansa and Theon have now escaped, so Ramsay established that there can only be one possible place of refuge for the two evaders: Castle Black, where Sansa's half-brother Jon Snow is Lord Commander of the Night's Watch...

Location:
Wolfswood, east of Winterfell, the North

During a rest break in the Wolfswood, Brienne tells Sansa that she had encountered her sister Arya some time ago, but she did not join her, and instead wanted to stay with her companion.

It is evident from Brienne's disappointed tone how much it is preying on her mind that she was unable to convince Arya to come with her and that she ultimately slipped away from her despite all the efforts she made in retrospect ("I spent three days looking for her. She disappeared.").

The Stark sisters were never particularly close to each other since both had completely different views of what their future lives should look like. While Sansa wanted to marry a rich lord later in life, Arya had it in her to become a warrior. However, her younger sister could be Sansa's last real blood relative and thus the last remaining piece of her family. So, the Stark girl is ultimately relieved when Brienne adds that she was safe and well at that encounter.

When Brienne subsequently asks about what happened in Winterfell, it takes some time for a thoughtful Sansa, who obviously finds it difficult to talk about the incidents that happened there, to find the right words.

She does not dare to tell Brienne what happened in detail, but she admits that it was a mistake to refuse her offer at the inn. ("I should have gone with you while I had the chance.").

This answer, which lacks details, makes it clear to an anxious Brienne that she was absolutely right to follow Sansa after their encounter at the inn in the Vale of Arryn (Episode 5.02 *The House of Black and White*) and also to disagree with Podrick's view that she was probably safe with the Boltons in Winterfell (Episode 5.05 *Kill the Boy*). It is quite obvious that appalling things happened within the castle. Beautiful memories the girl would not have kept secret...

Of course, Brienne had already assumed that Sansa was not in good company in Littlefinger's presence, otherwise she would not have made every effort to ride after her. But out of respect for the girl, as her new Lady, she does not reproach her for her rejection in retrospect, but rather she accepts and respects the "difficult choice" that Sansa had to make. After all, everyone faces difficult decisions at one time or another. Brienne could also reveal intimate secrets in this respect.

The small group intends to take the path towards Castle Black. Sansa's half-brother Jon Snow has been Lord Commander of the Night's Watch there for some time, and she could be safe from her sadistic husband Ramsay there for the time being. Unfortunately for Sansa, that is exactly where he suspects his wife is heading....

Nevertheless, one person has other plans: Theon. For fear that Jon may want to take revenge on him for his previous betrayal of the Starks, the heir of the Iron Islands considers it wiser to return home to his father.

Book of the Stranger

Location:
Castle Black, the North

Without Theon Greyjoy, who made his own way back to his old homeland, the Iron Islands, as previously mentioned, Sansa, Brienne and Podrick finally reach their destination in the far North: Castle Black.

A castle now held by no more than one hundred sworn brothers of the Night's Watch, which is located at the northern end of the Kingsroad and on the southern side of a gigantic fortification in the form of an ice wall, standing over 200 meters tall and almost 500 kilometers long.

Besides the Shadow Tower and Eastwatch-by-the-Sea, Castle Black is one of three manned strongholds (from an original nineteen) that protect the Seven Kingdoms from the dangers north of the Wall.

One of these dangers is the Free Folk. These so-called Wildlings live according to their own customs and laws and they have harbored deep-rooted hostility towards the inhabitants south of the Wall for many generations.

The intense, almost fixed gaze of Tormund Giantsbane, once a fierce opponent, but now a good friend of Jon Snow and also the leader of the Wildlings, towards Brienne and vice versa, when she slowly rides into the courtyard of the castle together with Sansa and Podrick, leave plenty of room for speculation. Does it appear that someone is expressing an interest in the tall woman, or is he just astonished that there are women of his size south of the Wall?

In any case, his probing gaze does not escape Brienne's attention, and one can now enjoy pondering whether she just keeps eye contact with him longer because he is fixated on her or whether she is surprised that she may have something of an admirer, even if it is "just" a Wildling. Who knows, who knows...

When the two half-siblings Sansa and Jon, who meanwhile were able to end his service in the Night's Watch (more detailed explanations on how this happened can be found on pages 203/204), see each other for the first time in a very long while, they fall into each other's arms with joy.

An embrace that cannot be taken for granted since Sansa never held her half-brother in high regard in contrast to her sister Arya. She never considered him a full member of the family during their childhood together in Winterfell and she always treated him contemptuously.

But in times when the Starks are almost eradicated, and she is still on the run from her sadistic husband Ramsay, Sansa obviously needs all the help she can get. Even if it only comes from her rather unloved half-brother...

Just like back then, when Brienne was in the service of Lady Stark and she reunited with her son Robb in his field camp (Episode 2.06 *The Old Gods and the New*), she again respectfully keeps her distance.

| Location: |
| **Castle Black, the North** |

In the courtyard of Castle Black, a loud conversation ensues between Davos Seaworth, Stannis Baratheon's closest adviser until his death, and Melisandre, the Red Priestess.

Since Stannis had decided on his way to Winterfell to send his loyal Davos half way back to Castle Black for supplies and to instead have the Red Woman still with him, Davos demands an explanation from the priestess as to what exactly happened in and around Winterfell.

But before she can say more than that there was a battle and Stannis was defeated, the two are suddenly interrupted by Brienne who spontaneously joins their conversation and tells them that she was there on the day when Stannis' army was beaten.

Davos is less than enthusiastic about Brienne's ungraceful, direct nature. When he politely but firmly tries to make it clear that she is talking to a knight and introduces himself as "Ser Davos Seaworth", she interrupts him again. She tells him in harsh terms that they had already met when she was a member of Renly Baratheon's Kingsguard before he was "assassinated with blood magic".

Brienne is alluding to the meeting of the two Baratheon brothers Renly and Stannis on the coast of the Stormlands (Episode 2.04 *Garden of Bones*).
All three of them attended that meeting, Brienne as a member of Renly's Kingsguard, and Melisandre and Davos as Stannis' closest confidants.

It becomes clear that Renly's death scenario is still ever-present for Brienne, despite her revenge taken on Stannis, noticeable from the burning glance she casts towards Melisandre in this moment. She is well aware of who caused the death of her former Lord, and the ominous words of the Red Priestess at the end of the dispute are obviously still ringing in her ears.

"Yes, it's in the past. It doesn't mean I forget. Or forgive."
- **Brienne to Davos Seaworth**

Davos senses that this topic is evidently agitating Brienne, but the blonde woman energetically objects to his rather timid attempt to categorize the whole issue as in the past and irreversible. Her pain at the loss of Renly is too deep, and thus she makes the two aware with a threatening undertone that she will neither forgive nor forget that moment. Her furious glance towards Melisandre, who is probably looking at the blonde woman almost guiltily because she has finally realized that she backed the wrong horse with Stannis, shows that she has no fear of the Red Woman. Nevertheless, Brienne had to find out what she is capable of.

This lack of concern continues when she takes some satisfaction in bluntly and bitterly telling the two that she personally executed Stannis Baratheon after he confessed his part in Renly's murder.

With this flippant confession, she was able to provoke the desire for revenge in both of Stannis' former allies. However, neither Davos nor Melisandre reproach her in this respect. Although Davos was one of Stannis' closest advisers, he was extremely skeptical of his relationship with the Red Woman from the outset since he feared that Stannis would rely too much on her witchcraft and lose sight of reality. Something that ultimately turned out to be correct.

In this respect, it must not be ignored that, until this point in time, Davos is unaware that Stannis sacrificed his own daughter Shireen, with whom he had an almost paternal relationship, to the flames upon Melisandre's prophecy to avoid starvation and secure victory over the Boltons. Should Davos ever become aware of this, I could imagine that he would never posthumously forgive Stannis for this, and Melisandre would then certainly feel his wrath. Whatever its nature...

I have long wondered how Brienne would react in a possible encounter with Davos Seaworth and Melisandre. I did know that she would confront the two after Renly's murder since it would not be in her nature to do anything else. The question was rather if she would only speak to them or would she call them both to account on the spot? Furthermore, since it was established at the end of the penultimate episode that Sansa's and thus also Brienne's path would lead to Castle Black, there was nothing standing in the way between a confrontation with Stannis' former allies. Provided, of course, that the screenwriters would not thwart the whole thing by having Davos and the priestess depart from Castle Black before Brienne's arrival. This would have been a real shame because this meeting and Brienne's purposeful and honest manner fully met my expectations. In my opinion, a one-on-one duel with Ser Davos would have detracted from the seriousness of this scene and made it seem somewhat unbelievable. Quite apart from the fact that our protagonist has also already taken her revenge.

Brienne eventually turns away from the two and leaves without saying a word. It would seem that the Lady of Tarth has no real interest in a further conversation. She only seized the opportunity to get her pent-up anger off her chest. Not just to anyone, but to precisely those who were very close to Stannis and who, in her eyes, are mainly to blame for Renly's murder. Her internal unrest allows her to throw all etiquette to the wind.

Even though Davos Seaworth was loyal to Stannis, he appears to show understanding, if not the deserved respect, for Brienne's behavior when he casts a thoughtful gaze towards her. Namely the fact that she killed his Lord to avenge her own. Above all, it helps to take into consideration that Davos was present for the "birth" of the deadly shadow and later strongly condemned this witchcraft. However, I do not think that he sees Brienne as a murderous monster but rather as a woman for whom honor and loyalty still mean something. Just like for him.

Location:
Castle Black, the North

Together with Jon Snow, Eddison Tollet, one of Jon's closest confidants in the brothers of the Night's Watch, as well as Tormund Giantsbane, Brienne, Sansa and Podrick eat a meal in the dining hall of Castle Black.

Even though Brienne is certainly not politely mannered, as comprehensively proven by the incident in the courtyard, despite her noble origin, she seems a little clueless with regard to the table manners of the Night's Watch. She may be aware of the rough customs so far in the North, especially when men are among her peers. Nevertheless, her almost helpless expression makes it appear as if she thinks it is in bad taste to eat noisily with bare hands despite having cutlery and feels out of place.

If there was a feeling at the beginning when Brienne rode into the courtyard of Castle Black with Sansa and Podrick, with Tormund gazing intensely at her, revealing that he may have found the woman to his liking, this is now confirmed.

The way he continuously eyes Brienne with interest or should I say: stares, while chewing on his leg of mutton, speaks volumes. Brienne briefly reciprocates Tormund's gaze, but it feels like the situation is extremely unpleasant for her which is why she looks away in embarrassment.

When examining the scene in detail, I somehow cannot imagine that it was a complete coincidence that Tormund sat diagonally opposite to Brienne at the table.... What a rascal!

The leader of the Wildlings is probably the first man in her life who actually makes genuine advances to Brienne, and it is a pity that she probably largely ignores this sympathy due to the prevailing view that the Wildlings are barbarians and uncivilized, as well as her previous bad experiences with men.

Her feelings for a certain Jaime Lannister may also prevent her from allowing more to happen.

Even if I personally hope, but somehow do not believe, that this possible romance will somehow continue and thus have a future, there would be something exotic about this love affair: the down-to-earth, hard-nosed nature boy from the far North, who certainly lacks the most refined manners, on the one side, and the virtuous and cultured noblewoman from the South on the other side. A tremendously delicate combination.

However, this amusing interaction between Tormund and Brienne almost steals the limelight from the real event in the scene – a letter from Winterfell from Ramsay Bolton to Jon Snow.

The new Lord of Winterfell and Warden of the North was right in his assumption that Sansa's path would lead her to the Wall and her half-brother. But the alternatives were also relatively clear...

Despite the fact that Ramsay's bastard status was lifted by royal decree some time ago, allowing him to bear the name "Bolton", he feared that he would lose all hereditary titles due to the birth of a legitimate son by Roose's new wife Walda, his stepmother. He, therefore, first murdered his father and threw the mother and newborn baby to his starving dogs shortly thereafter... As the sole heir , Ramsay is now Lord of Winterfell and may call himself Warden of the North.

In this letter, Ramsay calls for Jon to hand over his wife Sansa, otherwise he would not only retrieve her by force and allow his men to rape her, but he would also feed her youngest brother and thus Jon's half-brother Rickon, who is now in Ramsay's hands, to his dogs, and slaughter and flay alive all of the Wildlings under Jon's protection.

After the seizure of Winterfell by the Ironborn under Theon Greyjoy's leadership, Sansa's younger brothers

Bran and Rickon quickly managed to escape from the occupied castle with their direwolves, Summer and Shaggydog, and Osha, a Wildling woman in the service of the Starks, as well as Hodor, the mentally handicapped but gigantic stableman. On their way to the Wall and thus Rickon and Bran's half-brother Jon Snow, they made the acquaintance of siblings Jojen and Meera Reed who joined them.

However, the group subsequently separated. While Bran, his direwolf Summer, Hodor and the two Reed siblings continued towards the North, Osha, Rickon and his direwolf Shaggydog head for the Last Hearth, the seat of House Umber.

Until then, House Umber was a vassal House loyal to the Starks, and Bran considered this a safe place for his younger brother to stay.

After the fall of House Stark and due to their infuriation with the ever-growing number of Wildlings that Jon Snow allowed to pass through the Wall in his role as Lord Commander of the Night's Watch, the Umbers turned to the Boltons, who were now ruling the North, without making an oath of allegiance to them.

In order to demonstrate their loyalty, Smalljon Umber, the Lord of Last Hearth, handed Rickon and Osha over to Ramsay as a "gift", as well as the severed head of Rickon's direwolf as proof that he really was the youngest Stark offspring.

The Last Hearth, which was meant to be a refuge, proved to be a disastrous error in retrospect.

This is a serious threat with which Sansa ultimately convinces Jon, who initially wanted nothing to do with it in a previous conversation with his half-sister, to take back

Winterfell. After all, they could not only reclaim their home from the "monster" but they could also simultaneously free their brother or half-brother.

However, the 2000 Wildlings on their side that were classified as battle-ready by Tormund, do not appear to be a sufficient basis to cope with this plan.

During her conversation with Sansa in the Wolfswood (Episode 6.02 *Home*), Brienne suspected that Winterfell obviously must have been hell for her. And Ramsay's frightening and threatening words in this letter now provide the best proof that her feeling was correct: the new Warden of the North is anything but a nice guy.

Episode 6.05

The Door

ithin Castle Black, Sansa receives a letter from Petyr Baelish, in which he asks her for a face-to-face meeting in Mole's Town.

When Sansa and Brienne arrive in the village, which is not far from Castle Black and has become run-down and deserted after a Wildling raid, Littlefinger is already waiting for the Stark daughter. He seems a little surprised that the girl is not alone but she came accompanied by her protector. He had obviously asked her for a one-on-one meeting.

Bearing in mind Littlefinger's previous way of thinking and acting and the unscrupulousness and craftiness with which he pursues his objectives, which occasionally include the odd murder, Sansa's "precaution" is absolutely understandable.

In any case, Brienne would hardly have allowed Sansa to go alone. She has encountered Baelish and his shady and cunning manner more than once and, in her opinion, there are probably very few people in whose company the Stark girl would be in greater danger...

Sansa's reunion with her uncle-in-law is extremely frosty. It was ultimately he who had arranged her dreadful marriage to Ramsay Bolton, in which she had to endure unimaginable physical and mental pain. Baelish notices that Sansa is anything but sympathetic to him and tries to appease her and engage in damage limitation. Having heard that she had escaped from Winterfell, he immediately decided to come to her aid with the knights of the Vale of Arryn who found accommodation at Moat Cailin.

The girl does not address this offer in any detail but confronts the man with the question of whether he knew who or what Ramsay was. Without waiting for his answer, and with a petrified expression, she describes in some detail what Ramsay did to her on their wedding night.

As he is unable to find an answer when asked what else he thinks Ramsay did to her, and a longer silence fills the room, Brienne eventually sharply calls upon him to answer Sansa ("Lady Sansa asked you a question!").

Even if the tall woman is just a silent observer here, like at the very beginning of her storyline, she obviously listened to the conversation with suspicion, and the way she looks at Littlefinger as full of contempt and disgust the whole time speaks for itself.

Littlefinger admits that he made "a horrible mistake" with Ramsay Bolton and he did not have the slightest idea about all this, and he once again reaffirms that he wants to protect her, but these words do not restore confidence in his niece-in-law ("I don't believe you anymore. I don't need you anymore.").

Despite his confession to Ramsay in Episode 5.03 (*High Sparrow*) that he was almost a blank page for him ("I've heard very little about you, which makes you quite a rare thing as lords go."), it is really hard to believe that Baelish, who carefully plans every step down to the smallest detail and leaves nothing to chance, really knew or had heard nothing about Ramsay's sadistic streak. It, therefore, begs the question as to whether Littlefinger would have permitted the marriage if he had known all this, even at the risk of Sansa dying in the worst case? After all, Sansa was, in a way, the "key to the North" for Littlefinger and her death would mean him losing an extremely important trump card and in turn gaining a formidable opponent in the Boltons.

The fact that Brienne is by Sansa's side at this moment gives her a quite reasonable feeling of security, and thus she tells him that she could order her protector to cut him down then and there. An instruction that she probably would have given if she had a similar moral threshold to Littlefinger.
Instead, Sansa simply makes it clear to Baelish that she will take back the North with her brother and that she never wants to see him again.

But before Littlefinger bids her farewell, he gives her the tip to secure the support of House Tully. Her great uncle Brynden Tully has now recaptured Riverrun, the Tullys' family seat, from Walder Frey and amassed a powerful army – a good option for her plan to take back Winterfell...

After the death of Hoster Tully (Sansa's maternal grandfather), the murder of her mother Catelyn (née Tully), the imprisonment of her uncle Edmure (Tully) in the course of the Red Wedding, as well as the death of her aunt Lysa Arryn (also née Tully), Riverrun fell under the control of House Frey by royal decree. Only Brynden Tully, Sansa's grumpy great uncle, who ironically gave himself the nickname "Blackfish" due to his controversial attitude towards life, was able to escape the massacre at the Twins by a fortunate coincidence. He managed to form an army and recapture Riverrun.

Even now in the certainty that he has definitely lost his niece-in-law, Baelish's craftiness is recognizable. By subtly adding that Jon is only her half-brother and not her real brother at the end of Sansa's rejection of his assistance, he quickly tries to drive a wedge between her and Jon and create distrust in his usual cunning way.

Even though Sansa could use every possible help in the fight against the Boltons and their allies, she eventually refuses Littlefinger's support and thus the knights of the Vale of Arryn. One might think that this was negligent. Sure, but understandable from Sansa's point of view.

How could she trust a man whose deviousness has not only caused so much suffering to her but also to other people, and who made her a pawn in his own personal agenda?

It seems far more appropriate to trust her half-brother and his allies, even if this motley bunch of Wildlings and brothers of the Night's Watch appear to be outnumbered by the Boltons and their vassals.

During a briefing regarding the further course of action and how Winterfell will be recaptured from the Boltons, Brienne is also present. She is only a silent observer, but attentive as usual.

Above all, Davos Seaworth now appears to be a valuable aid and his knowledge of war strategy provides the first evidence of why he was one of Stannis Baratheon's closest advisers.

Unlike Sansa, who at least still sees the Karstarks as a possible and powerful ally out of all the possible larger houses of the North, Davos has reasonable doubts about being able to get them on their side. After all, Sansa's now murdered brother Robb executed the head of the family, Lord Rickard Karstark, a long time ago, whereupon the Karstarks broke their oath of allegiance to the Starks and joined the Boltons (see reviews on pages 82 and 175).

Despite the fact that the Umbers, another large house of the North, have now joined the Boltons and delivered Sansa's youngest brother Rickon to Ramsay as a sign of confidence, there are still enough smaller houses to win over for their cause, as Sansa's half-brother Jon rightly points out on the military strategy table. He states that "they equal the others" together with the smaller houses.

Sansa, therefore, places her hopes in the Stark family name and its power which alone should be sufficient to mobilize all remaining houses. When she eventually mentions the Tullys, who are "no Northerners", but who she is sure would support her in her fight against the Boltons, Davos is surprised to learn that the Tullys have an army again after losing Riverrun.
Instead of giving Jon an honest answer when he asks her how she knows this, she lies to him by saying that Ramsay received a raven with this information before she escaped Winterfell...

This is an obviously plausible explanation for all the others seated at the table, with the exception of Brienne, who of course knows the true source of information regarding the newly formed Tully army, and one more reason for Davos to believe in the victory over the Boltons ("That's good. The Blackfish is a legend. His support would mean a great deal.").

Above all, it is interesting to see Brienne's facial expression and reaction in this respect. Initially curious to know what the answer of the girl to her left would be to Jon's persistent questioning about where she got her information, she turns away disappointed by Sansa's lie. This dishonesty is probably devastating for someone like Brienne who considers honesty to be a basic virtue. Especially coming from the woman whom she has promised to protect. But, of course, she remains silent. After all, as a loyal companion, one does not undermine one's Lady and jeopardize her newly gained trust in the spur of the moment.

The question remains as to why Sansa lied to her half-brother and thus all those involved? In my opinion, there is an entirely plausible explanation for this:

Although Mole's Town is just a few miles away from Castle Black, it is hard to believe that Jon would have allowed Sansa to leave the castle, neither alone nor accompanied. And certainly not in the present situation with the ever-present predicament with the Boltons.
Consequently, Sansa will have made her way to the small village without Jon's consent, with only Brienne for her protection. This, in turn, means that she would now have to be accountable for putting her life in danger so frivolously. If Jon would have known about Sansa's conversation with Littlefinger, he would have been able to simply ask her what had come of it. However, the name Littlefinger is not mentioned at the table, and only Sansa knows why.

What also struck me in this scene: Ser Davos and priestess Melisandre show absolutely no hostility to Brienne, not even in the form of dirty looks. The two former Stannis supporters have obviously resigned themselves to this new situation.

Sansa's proposal to incorporate the Tully army in their plan is met with great approval by all those involved.

Only Sansa's request to send Brienne to the Riverlands for the necessary negotiations with her great uncle Brynden is met with opposition from the tall woman. She ultimately vowed to protect Sansa.

However, Sansa vehemently rejects Brienne's immediate counterproposal to send a raven with a message to Riverrun in her stead. The risk is too great that Ramsay could intercept it and thus ruin their plans.

The Stark daughter insists that Brienne takes this mission into her own hands and thus obviously places great faith in her negotiation skills ("My uncle will talk to you and you'll know how to talk to him.").

However, eloquence is not necessarily one of Brienne's key skills. Expectations are high as to how her discussion with the Blackfish will progress – should she ever reach Riverrun...

Brienne's subsequent concerned look when the two are eventually alone together in Sansa's chamber does not go unnoticed by the Stark girl. Thus, when prompted, the blonde woman ultimately admits that she would not like to leave her alone.

Above all, Brienne is caused discomfort by the prospect of leaving the girl with Davos Seaworth and the Red Woman, hence, abandoning her in the company of those who helped Stannis Baratheon "murder his own brother", who then looked "for a leader with better prospects" like cowardly opportunists in the face of impending defeat, and thus left their Lord high and dry.

As a principled person, it seems absolutely incomprehensible to her as to how Sansa could have confidence in such people in her current situation.

In my opinion, both judgements are accurate to a limited extent:
Melisandre actually made off after Selyse Baratheon's suicide and before Stannis' desperate attack on Winterfell since she evidently became aware that he was not the "chosen one", as suggested to her by the flames.

After Stannis burned his own daughter Shireen at the stake upon Melisandre's prophecy, his wife Selyse hanged herself. On the one hand, this was certainly out of grief and despair for the loss of her own daughter and, on the other, out of anger at herself for unconditionally following the Red Woman and her faith in the Lord of Light to ultimately see it all come to nothing. Or should I say: to a funeral pyre?

However, the fact that Melisandre subsequently ran away to Castle Black was not due to her desire to join a new savior. In fact, she was certainly driven by the fear of possibly falling into the hands of the Boltons or being held accountable for the ultimately meaningless burning of Shireen by surviving Baratheon followers.

In contrast, the situation is very different for Davos. If Stannis had not sent him back to the Wall halfway to Winterfell to replenish the gradually declining food reserves, he would have loyally followed him to his death during the attack on Winterfell. But as we know, Stannis went on without him and sent Davos back to Castle Black.

Furthermore, Davos already condemned the birth of the shadow that ultimately became Renly's downfall. If he had seen an opportunity to prevent this act at that time, he would probably have done so. Thus, it is only right to blame him for the murder to a certain extent.

It is just as unfortunate for Davos that Brienne quite clearly goes by the saying "In for a penny, in for a pound" and the motto "He who does not prevent injustice is as bad as the guilty man".

However, Brienne must be given credit for the fact that so far nobody has been able to change her mind in this respect and thus she only has this one view of things.

Even with regards to Tormund, the tall woman is absolutely uncertain about what she should think of him. In any case, it seems like "that Wildling fellow with the beard" has completely put her off her stride with his continuous non-verbal infatuation as she goes on with a slightly hysterical tone. Since she was treated dreadfully by men in her childhood, she initially sees virtually all men as the personification of evil and approaches them with deep mistrust.

Considering all the suffering, deviousness and cruelty that she has experienced or at least heard about during her lifetime emanating from Littlefinger, the Boltons or Locke, it is perhaps understandable that her faith in an honest world of men seems to be all but destroyed. She even notoriously had problems with Jaime Lannister from the outset, and it took a long time until she could develop trust with him.

"Then why did you lie to him when he asked you how you learned about Riverrun?" - **Brienne to Sansa Bolton**

When Sansa answers Brienne by stating that Jon is her brother, who will surely protect her, no matter what, and that she trusts him, it takes a moment for her protector to pluck up the courage and confront Sansa with the question as to why she lied to her brother in relation to Riverrun, despite supposedly trusting him.

This question from the tall woman is more than justified, but Sansa has no answer. In this respect, from the Stark girl's perspective, it would have been completely unproblematic to tell her protector that she would not have been able to admit to her half-brother that she left Castle Black without permission if she wanted to keep her little secret to herself. After all, Brienne was with her in Mole's Town and she knows why they were there and what was said. However, Sansa does not say anything. She remains silent. Perhaps because she has now realized that it was wrong to keep Jon in the dark. Perhaps she feels caught "on the wrong foot" by Brienne's direct manner and energetic scrutiny and she does not dare to admit it.
Like a few times before, these assumptions remain a matter for conjecture.

It is also brave of Brienne to address her new Lady so directly. If someone like this woman places such an increased emphasis on virtues, it is no wonder that it comes pouring out of her like at the meeting with Davos and Melisandre. After all, she waits until she is alone with Sansa to ask this delicate question. On the other hand, she can well and truly antagonize other people with this spontaneous action and even literally leave Sansa speechless, as she does in this case.

The fact that Brienne is slightly grouchy about her imposed mission to consult with Sansa's great uncle seems understandable since she primarily offered the girl her protection with her oath. She certainly did not have conducting negotiations in mind, but perhaps she should have simply paid closer attention to her job description...

There is a good pinch of humor for the viewer in the closing scene when the entire entourage arrives in the courtyard of Castle Black ready to march shortly thereafter.

Even though her path will lead them in different directions, while Brienne and Podrick will head south to Riverrun, and Jon, Sansa and Tormund will attempt to mobilize allies in the North to take back Winterfell, as luck would have it, Brienne and Tormund are sitting next to each other, on horseback.

I think this scene can be enjoyed by practically everyone when the Wildling and Brienne's eyes meet for a short moment, Tormund again visibly adores her and Brienne then fretfully looks away, rolling her eyes.

The question arises as to whether she really is as irritated by him as she seems or whether she is just doing it to protect herself.

As previously mentioned, here are a few words of explanation regarding the question as to why Jon Snow was able to leave the Night's Watch even though he is a sworn member:

By taking the vows, each recruit of the Night's Watch relinquishes all claims of ownership by birthright and abstains from starting a family and having children from that moment and for the rest of their life. Although members of the Night's Watch are not forbidden from seeing their parents or siblings, they require the consent of the Lord Commander for this. Desertion is not tolerated and punished by death.
The Night's Watch is "non-partisan" and thus does not serve any single Lord, but exists solely to protect the realm from the dangers that lie beyond the Wall.
Of course, as a sworn member of the Night's Watch, all of the abovementioned points also applied to Jon Snow, especially after his appointment to Lord Commander.
When Jon allowed the Wildlings to leave their homeland north of the Wall to settle the lands south of the Wall in the face of the imminent danger in the form of the "White

Walkers", an army of mystical creatures that had actually long been defeated, some of the "black brothers" conspired against him.

These members saw Jon's actions as fraternizing with the enemy and the disregard of millennia of traditions that have always regarded the Wildlings as enemies of the Seven Kingdoms.

Consequently, a few of these "hardliners" murdered Jon Snow by multiple stab wounds. Jon's sworn oath also ended when he died.

However, Melisandre's supernatural abilities as the Red Priestess brought him back to life shortly thereafter. As a "reborn" and free man, he sentenced all the conspirators and (somehow) murderers, who were imprisoned thanks to the support of the Wildlings, to death by hanging.

He provisionally handed over his now vacant position as Lord Commander to Eddison Tollet, one of his closest friends among the black brothers.

The Broken Man

> **Location:**
> **somewhere in an unspecified location in the Riverlands**

After Arya Stark left the heavily wounded Hound to die after his lost duel against Brienne at the end of season four (Episode 4.10 *The Children*), the subsequent fate of the uncouth warrior was not clear for a long time.
Would he succumb to his injuries or would he be rescued by a random passer-by?

The opening sequence of this seventh episode finally provides the answer to this question: Yes, Sandor, the Hound Clegane, actually survived!

Ray, a former soldier who renounced violence a long time ago and is now a homeless septon, who preaches the Faith of the Seven without his own sept, found the doomed Sandor and nursed him back to health, despite his almost hopeless condition.

Feeling strengthened again, the Hound now actively supports the other members of Ray's small and peaceful faith community with the completion of a sept in the middle of nowhere in the Riverlands.

When Brother Ray watches Sandor chopping wood, he is deeply impressed by his strength and the ease with which he splits the logs.

The septon would not believe that this colossus bursting with strength was not mauled by several men, as he initially assumed, but by a single person. However, the Hound promptly corrects Ray's expressed assumption that this man "must have been some kind of monster" by stating that the supposed "he" was a woman. The septon cannot stifle a small laugh at this answer. It seems inconceivable to him that this giant man has actually been defeated by a woman.

Of course, it is clear who this woman was, and it is a sign of greatness that the Hound so frankly admits this to the septon. He could have ultimately sugar-coated this indignity for his benefit and asserted that he was attacked, robbed and left for dead by a horde of scoundrels, and everyone would have readily accepted it.

The way in which the Hound angrily hacks at the wood in front of him following his statement suggests that the lost duel against Brienne is still getting to him. Whether this thought has now created a desire for revenge in him or whether the near-death experience has perhaps turned Sandor into a peaceful person, who has left his wild and brutal side behind, will likely be revealed in the future...

No One

Location:
before the gates of Riverrun, Riverlands

ollowing Sansa's order to persuade her great uncle Brynden, the "Blackfish", Tully to support her in taking back Winterfell with his army, Brienne and Podrick finally reach Riverrun, the family seat of the Tullys.

Unfortunately, the two could not have chosen a worse time for their trip to the Riverlands since the castle is currently, quite clearly under siege.

After Joffrey's death, his younger brother Tommen ascended the Iron Throne – and thus also a son born of Cersei and Jaime's incest. Insurmountable differences with King Tommen ultimately meant that he relieved Jaime Lannister from his position as Lord Commander of the Kingsguard, but he was also released from the Kingsguard. In order to remain in the service of the crown, he receives the order to support the Freys in taking back Riverrun with the Lannister army (see review on page 194).

Brienne's acute observation that Podrick has "a keen military mind", when he recognizes the many tents in front of the castle as a siege would probably not have sounded much different before the key scene in Episode 5.03 (*High Sparrow*), which is virtually the turning point of their mutual relationship. Of course, there is irony resonating in this answer. However, in my view, it is more of a friendly teasing in the sense of "well, it's probably not the weekly market", and not her intention to make her companion look like a fool in a sarcastic manner. Why should she? Since that day by the campfire, Podrick has given her no more reasons to disparage him.

However, Brienne is simply not a comedian and probably the most humorless person in the Seven Kingdoms. Even witty remarks (Sorry, what?) sound like eulogies or quotes from a textbook.

When the woman suddenly sees Jaime Lannister riding through the Lannister camp from her position, it appears that the wistfulness in her gaze and her misty eyes are abruptly caused by old memories of their initially painful but later pleasant time together.

Podrick's multiple attempts ("My lady! My lady!") to draw the attention of his companion, who is wallowing in the past, to the fact that Lannister soldiers have now noticed her presence and are approaching, are unsuccessful. She is too deep in thought and seems to have completely blanked out everything else around her.

Only when one of the soldiers sharply addresses her, wanting to know who she is and what she is doing, her stoic gaze gradually moves away from the camp and she is torn from her dreams.

With both feet back on the ground, she makes it unmistakably clear to the Lannister soldier that she, Brienne of Tarth, wishes to speak with "Ser Jaime Lannister" – and that she has his sword...

The fact that she mentions the sword here, which Jaime expressly gave her at that time (Episode 4.04 *Oathkeeper*), after a brief moment of reflection, raises a number of questions that will hopefully be answered shortly...

Location:
Jaime Lannister's camp before the gates of Riverrun, Riverlands

---

While Brienne and Jaime meet again in his tent, a reunion not considered possible, Podrick unexpectedly encounters another old acquaintance: Bronn.

Tyrion's bodyguard, who is now in the service of his brother Jaime following his arrest, is more than surprised to see the former squire and cupbearer of his small-statured

Lord again since he actually believed he would be "dead by now".

No matter what topic, Bronn is not necessarily known for his restraint but he will happily cut straight to the point. This is the case in this scene.

Therefore, his crude and filthy question to Podrick at the beginning of the scene ("You think they're fucking?"), as to whether the former Lord Commander of the Kingsguard, who is in charge of the siege, is pursuing his carnal desires with the tall woman, does not come as a surprise to Brienne's companion, but it clearly shows him that the former mercenary's attitude towards women has not changed after such a long time.

Bronn, who indulges in a liberal lifestyle, still primarily sees women as objects for satisfying men's sexual desires. Furthermore, this man, who is somehow always surrounded by the aura of a bar brawler, is still of the opinion that there will inevitably be intimate relations between a man and a woman as soon as they are in the same room together. But Brienne's squire by no means agrees, and certainly not with regard to his companion. He knows the woman and her experiences with men during her lifetime only too well.

Jaime would probably rather grow a new right hand than sleep with Brienne. What's more, Bronn's pompous announcement that he would "fuck" Brienne if he were in Jaime's place also seems rather shaky. I think the woman would have the right non-verbal answer for him in this case. And deservedly so.

We have ultimately come to know Brienne as someone who blanks out everything that has nothing to do with her mission – sexual relations included. However, a certain degree of shame on her part in combination with inexperience and her non-existing interest in sex cannot simply be dismissed in this respect.

Podrick makes it clear to Bronn that absolutely nothing would happen between the Kingslayer and the Lady of Tarth on a sexual level, despite the present opportunity, and dismisses his subsequent sharp-tongued remarks that Podrick has a "magic cock" and that he "must have shown it to her by now".

As a reward for Podrick saving Tyrion's life at the Battle of the Blackwater, his Lord treated him to a night in a brothel with several prostitutes and the required cash. When Podrick returned some time later with all the cash, both Bronn and Tyrion were utterly astounded. His "art of love" was obviously so satisfying that the women did not want payment...

Unlike Bronn, the boy sees Brienne for what she really is: an excellent and disciplined warrior with strengths and weaknesses who is teaching him horseback riding and the intelligent use of the sword as her squire.

No more, no less.

A statement that seems to shake Bronn's macho world-view. Are there actually women who not only serve the purpose of bringing pleasure to men? Bronn's dumb-founded "Is she? Oh!" suggests at least this.

Location:
Jaime Lannister's camp before the gates of Riverrun, Riverlands

---

Of course, Podrick was correct in his view that it "only" came to an exchange of words between the Kingslayer Jaime Lannister and Brienne and not, as Bronn assumed, to the exchange of bodily fluids. However, in light of Brienne's previous patterns of behavior, her restraint was more likely than exuberant joy (or more).

Brienne's sudden appearance at his camp takes Jaime by surprise since he really did not expect that her mission to find Sansa would actually be a success. He even assumed that the Stark girl was already dead since in his opinion "girls like her don't live very long". This statement slightly provokes Brienne. She has ultimately been ensuring the Stark daughter's protection for quite some time.

Brienne has heard enough about the cruel things that the girl had to experience at a young age, from Sansa herself and other third parties.

Starting with her father's beheading, then the murder of her mother and brother Robb at the Twins, and finally her forced marriages, first to Tyrion Lannister and then later to Ramsay Bolton, who also abused and imprisoned her. The murder of her aunt Lysa at the Eyrie should also be noted, even if the viewer did not necessarily have the feeling that the aunt and niece were very close.

If Sansa did not have this unconditional will to survive, she would have probably been mentally broken following the rape by Ramsay on her wedding night. Fortunately, she pulled herself out of this dilemma and proved her strength by escaping from Winterfell. Jaime seems to deny this characteristic to almost all women, present company excluded. Brienne's angry response that she does not believe he knows "many girls like her" is therefore understandable.

Despite this minor dissonance, Jaime is impressed by Brienne's achievement and he gives her his honest praise for fulfilling her oath sworn to Catelyn Stark ("Well, I'm proud of you. I am."), even if he probably would have preferred not to have received this news from Brienne in the current situation during the siege of Riverrun.

After the Blackfish was able to take back his family seat from the Freys, they requested military support from the Lannisters to recapture the castle. Nevertheless, Sansa's great uncle has no intention of abandoning the stronghold despite the numerical superiority of the enemy. Thus, a siege of Riverrun should therefore bring a speedy end to this troublesome matter.

His sister Cersei still suspects Sansa of being jointly responsible for King Joffrey's murder, and she still wishes the Stark daughter dead because of it. Jaime once again reminds Brienne of this extremely problematic conflict ultimately also making the woman the center of attention for the Lannisters including him theoretically since she is now in the service of the sought-after girl.

Brienne's presence could not be any more inappropriate. Thus, Jaime's subsequent question to Brienne in a slightly agitated tone, "What the hell are you doing here?", is probably meant less as a reproach but rather more as an expression of genuine concern for her safety since the situation could escalate relatively soon, and it could lead to a battle if the Blackfish does not give in.

When Brienne tells Jaime that the Blackfish is the actual reason for her presence in the Riverlands and that she intends to persuade him and his army to ride north with her to help his grandniece Sansa take back Winterfell from the Boltons, it becomes increasingly clear that the former Lord Commander of the Kingsguard and the tall woman are now in opposing camps.

Unlike Jaime, who sees the Tullys as "rebels" who have unlawfully taken over Riverrun, Brienne is of the opinion that these so-called rebels are only trying to defend their homeland against those who were once awarded the stronghold by order of King Joffrey "as a reward for betraying Robb Stark and slaughtering his family" at the Red Wedding. In light of her embittered facial expression and the resoluteness in her voice, it is evident how affected she is by this injustice.

The description of people, who were initially robbed of their homeland who are taking it back and now standing against those who want to take it away again, as "rebels", seems downright grotesque and does not comply with Brienne's understanding of justice or fairness at all. Especially considering that the Freys were heavily to blame for the bloodbath at the Twins and, to make matters worse, Riverrun was passed to them by royal decree.

In view of her expression, the attitude of her conversation partner is a tremendous disappointment for Brienne. She probably would have expected this comment from any other Lannister commander, but not from Jaime. He makes her aware of his unyielding position on this matter.

Jaime ultimately ends the long silence caused by the deadlock by calmly persuading Brienne to stop arguing about politics. This is an interesting parallel to their initial dispute in the Harrenhal bathhouse (Episode 3.05 *Kissed by Fire*) when Jaime calmed down a conversation that was about to spin out of control.

But, of course, politics cannot be completely kept out of things. The mission that led Brienne to Riverrun in the first place is ultimately something of a political matter.

The woman is well aware that the current siege of Riverrun substantially hampers her actual mission. However, quite contrary to her nature that often makes her actions hasty and thus not always intelligent and correct, she demonstrates her strategic abilities. In order to avoid any unnecessary bloodshed and to end the siege peacefully, she appeals to Jaime's honor as a knight and requests that she be allowed "to enter Riverrun under a flag of truce". She wanted to try to persuade the Blackfish to give up the stronghold, so that Jaime can peacefully seize the castle with his troops. In return, he should grant the Tullys safe passage to the North.

A classic win-win situation: she would have fulfilled her duty, and the castle gates would be opened for the Lannisters and the Freys. In this respect, the only loser would be Sansa's great uncle. And he has not yet given the impression that he has any interest in giving up the castle without resistance. A delicate starting position...

It is precisely in Brynden Tully that Jaime sees the crux that could doom Brienne's plan to failure and makes him strongly doubt the success of the proposal. He already had one unsuccessful conversation with the "old goat", as he disrespectfully calls the Blackfish due to his stubbornness. However, not even the threat of Edmure Tully's execution, Brynden's nephew, who has been held captive by the Freys since the Red Wedding, can persuade him to surrender. How should Brienne perform the feat of convincing someone who is, in Jaime's opinion, "even more stubborn" than her, to give up the castle?
In this context, it is remarkable that Brynden Tully accepts the death of his nephew with a shrug of the shoulders to hold Riverrun, even though the Tully words are "Family, Duty, Honor" and family takes priority over everything else.

"Hang him and be done with it." - **Brynden Tully to Jaime Lannister (Episode 6.07** *The Broken Man***)**

Typical Blackfish – he didn't give himself this nickname for no good reason – he simply swaps the given parameters and thus clearly shows his first priority: HONOR.

In the run-up to the Red Wedding massacre at the Twins, where Robb Stark, his wife Talisa and her unborn baby, as well as his mother Catelyn were murdered among others, Edmure Tully married Roslyn Frey, one of Walder Frey's many daughters. Catelyn Stark's brother, who agreed to the marriage as a "replacement" for his nephew Robb Stark, escaped death at this bloodbath, but he was captured by the Freys.

With Edmure, they held leverage over the Starks and the Tullys, which they were ready to use for their own purposes.

So, it is Brienne's stubbornness, previously addressed by Jaime that ultimately makes him cave in. He gives her his word that the Tullys will be granted safe passage and he allows her a deadline until nightfall for her plan that does not sound at all promising.

Barely made this concession to her, Brienne surprisingly unfastens her sword belt.

"You gave it to me for a purpose. I've achieved that purpose." - **Brienne to Jaime Lannister**

When she goes to return Oathkeeper to him, the sword made from Valyrian steel that he presented to her shortly before the start of her mission, stating that it fulfilled its purpose, he is extremely perplexed.

She apparently really felt that the sword entrusted to her was a temporary loan for this certain mission, and as dutiful and honest as she is, she now intends to return it to him. Furthermore, solely the determination with which she counters him with the sword shows Jaime that Brienne is not joking.

He, therefore, reaffirms his former statement that the sword is hers – forever ("It's yours. It will always be yours.").

After Brienne's consequent long gaze into Jaime's eyes, who eventually makes her realize that he is absolutely serious about what he said, she takes Oathkeeper back.

Considering that Valyrian steel is priceless, Jaime's gesture of giving Brienne this precious sword for the rest of her life proves one thing, above all: how much this woman means to him.

"Should I fail to persuade the Blackfish to surrender and if you attack the castle, honor compels me to fight for Sansa's kin. (…) To fight you."
- **Brienne to Jaime Lannister**

Just before she goes to leave the tent, she pauses and tells Jaime in clear but slightly depressing words that the failure of her plan and a possible attack on the castle would force her to unite with the Blackfish and thus against him - against Jaime - due to her oath.

Even now, at this moment, which could point the way for their paths, their gazes constantly fixed on each other, the viewer realizes what the two feel for one another and that only their loyalty to their respective clients, or rather Jaime's love for his sister Cersei, stands between them and forces them to hold back their emotions.

Of course, Jaime knows that he would not stand a chance in a one-on-one duel against Brienne due to the loss of his sword hand and that, in the worst-case scenario, she would kill him for the sake of honor which she puts before her personal needs, despite her feelings for him. His subsequent statement that it will hopefully not come to a battle is hardly surprising and highlights his fear of being killed in this battle himself or being responsible for Brienne's death. Something that he would never forgive as things stand at present.

The fact that Brienne then quickly vanishes from Jaime's tent without any parting words seems to be a protective reaction on her part rather than the desire to leave as fast as possible. The likelihood of being overwhelmed by her feelings and bursting into tears in the end would be too high, a reaction that she is probably not willing to admit - neither herself nor Jaime, and an emotional balancing act which is roughly comparable with the farewell scenes in Harrenhal (Episode 3.07 *The Bear and the Maiden Fair*) and King's Landing (Episode 4.04 *Oathkeeper*).

Jaime watches her leave for a short moment in the knowledge that they will probably face each other as enemies when they next meet.

The encounters between Brienne and Jaime somehow always remind me of the popular ballad about "The Two Kings' Children" who also cannot be together. I suppose I am probably not the only one.

Of course, once again, this emotional farewell scene is accompanied by Ramin Djawadi's "The Old Gods and the New" from the moment Brienne goes to return Oathkeeper to Jaime through to her departure from the tent.

Location:
Riverrun, Riverlands

Brienne's attempt to persuade the Blackfish to give up his family seat goes exactly how Jaime previously assumed during their discussion.

Indeed, Sansa's great uncle Brynden is just as stubborn as Brienne, and he sees no reason to leave the castle to the Lannisters and Freys without a fight.

Even Brienne's desperate mention that she has a letter signed by his grandniece has no impact and cannot change his mind ("I don't know her signature. I don't know you. And I will not surrender. (...) If you think I'm abandoning my family's seat on the Kingslayer's word of honor you're a bloody fool!").

Brienne has already been able to gain experience in comparable situations with her two independent attempts to convince the two Stark daughters to come with her. Neither of these attempts were successful, as is well known.

The Blackfish vigorously rejects Brienne's objection that Riverrun will not be able to withstand the siege for long. There is no lack of food reserves.

When, in the same breath, Brynden Tully calls Jaime Lannister Brienne's "one-handed friend" in allusion to his missing sword hand, since he not only allowed the woman to cross the siege line, but she also carries this valuable and eye-catching sword, she strongly objects. She in no way considered him to be her friend.

Even if Brienne obviously has a strong emotional attachment to Jaime, terms such as "friend" or "friendship" do not seem like words that she uses frivolously.

And she does well not to. With all the ever-changing alliances, conspiracies and other intrigues, which not only has she witnessed so far, but also the viewer, who would you want to wholeheartedly call a "friend"?

Jaime Lannister may well be an attractive and desirable man to Brienne. But a friend? In my (and probably her) opinion, their moral principles and values are too different for them to be friends. So far, at least...

The repeated mention of her sword Oathkeeper in this scene is remarkable. Having served the purpose of fulfilling her mission, it now seems like more of a curse than a blessing.
Both the Hound (Episode 4.10 *The Children*) and Petyr Baelish (Episode 5.02 *The House of Black and White*) believed Brienne was in the service of the Lannisters during their encounters with her due to the sword decorated with Lannister gold. And in both cases, the Valyrian steel was significantly responsible for her ultimate failure. Thus, the Blackfish is the third person to notice and criticize it.

"Ser Jaime kept his word to your niece Catelyn Stark. He sent me to find Sansa, to help her as Catelyn wanted. He gave me this sword to protect her. That is what I have done and I will continue to do until the day I die!"
- **Brienne to Brynden Tully**

With a verbal counterattack, which is impressive by Brienne's standards, she eventually manages to get the "old goat" to at least take a look at the letter, she was holding before his nose the whole time.
Perhaps Brynden Tully is surprised by Brienne's stubbornness. However, he is ultimately impressed and convinced by the determination that she brings her and Jaime's oath to his niece Catelyn and thus the importance of her sword into play.

However, the initial hint of satisfaction on Brienne's face that she is getting closer to her mission objective is shattered once again when the Blackfish apologetically tells her that he does not have enough men to capture Winterfell.

Although he has understanding for his grandniece's request, Riverrun is his home in the same way as Winterfell is hers, and he is not willing to simply leave it to Jaime Lannister

I personally doubt that a sufficient number of men would have convinced the Blackfish to send them north. His homeland simply meant too much to him.

When he gives the letter back to Brienne and bids her farewell with a short nod, there is the feeling that the rug has once again been pulled out from under her feet. Her contemplative, almost resigned look seems to confirm this. Her streak of bad luck will simply not go away!

It can now be speculated as to whether it was wise of Sansa to entrust Brienne, who is certainly not one of the most adept people when it comes to diplomacy and empathy, with this task. Indeed, the Blackfish is also an extremely unruly and tough negotiator and was a tough nut to crack for Jaime Lannister who is never at a loss for words.

Despite this disappointing result, I am of the opinion that Brienne could make her way back to Sansa with her head held high.

It speaks volumes for Brienne that she does not blame her targets or adverse circumstances for her failure, as in the previous encounters with the two Stark girls and, above all, Renly's murder she had to idly witness, but rather she takes responsibility on herself when she eventually calls on Po-

drick to find a maester to send a raven to Sansa – a raven
with the simple message that she has "failed".

Heck! You just want to take her in your arms and tell her:
"Hey, it's not your fault. You did your best. Chin up, girl!
You will have luck on your side at some point! Your journey is far from over!". Until now, she has always managed
to recover from these setbacks. Why not this time, too? She
will certainly have enough opportunities to lose the tag of
a "walking failure"...

Location:
Riverrun, Riverlands

Edmure Tully, Catelyn Stark's younger brother and son of
Hoster Tully, was imprisoned by the Freys at the Red
Wedding and they have held him captive since then.
Jaime Lannister then found the rightful heir of Riverrun
effectively leverage the Tullys, who were able to recapture
the stronghold from the Freys, to surrender and thus
swiftly end the siege of the castle. However, the Blackfish,
Edmure's uncle and deputy commander of Riverrun during his absence, refused to give up his home despite the

prospect of Edmure's execution. Since Brienne's attempt to change his mind by the agreed time was unsuccessful, Jaime used a daring ploy. He realized that the Blackfish would apparently send his nephew to his doom without batting an eyelash to keep his family seat.

A realization that made it clear to him that there was obviously a very tense relationship between uncle and nephew.

Since Edmure is the rightful Lord of Riverrun, unlike his uncle Brynden, Jaime was confident that the forces within the fortress felt committed to him, and not the Blackfish. With the threat of murdering his son, conceived on his wedding night, Jaime allowed Edmure to go the castle gate and demand entry. A move that actually worked out. The Tully captain saw Edmure as his rightful Lord and asserted himself, despite strong resistance from the Blackfish, who sensed a trap by the Kingslayer, due to the soldiers standing behind him and he eventually allowed Edmure to pass. A disastrous mistake. Having barely arrived inside the stronghold, Edmure immediately ordered his subordinate soldiers to lay down their weapons and surrender the castle to the Lannisters and the Freys without resistance. He even wanted to hand over his unloved uncle Brynden to the enemy and went looking for him...

The Blackfish was absolutely right in his assumption that Edmure's sudden release and his demand for the drawbridge to be lowered and the gate to be opened would be a trap by the besiegers.

While the Tullys surrender to the Frey and Lannister forces marching into the castle, the Blackfish leads Brienne and Podrick to the lower catacombs of the castle to a rowboat moored there as a means of escape. Thus, he offers them a way to avoid being captured and secretly escape the occupied castle. The fact that Riverrun was ideally built where the Red Fork of the Trident meets the Tumblestone proves to be an exceptionally advantageous phenomenon.

Brienne's plan to persuade the Blackfish to surrender peacefully before dusk failed, and thus she considered her deal with Jaime to be invalid. Of course, the respectful and possibly even amicable relationship between the two still exists. And I think the viewer would not be surprised if Jaime would not consider the woman to be an enemy, despite her presence in the castle, but let her go solely because of his feelings for her. Yet, Brienne is an extremely principled person. The agreement was only valid until nightfall. No later. Subsequently, everything would be the same, which means a state of war and siege. According to her reasoning, she would be nothing more than a defeated enemy. So as not to rely too heavily on Jaime's affection towards her, her only remaining option is to escape. Better safe than sorry...

Brienne already showed this somehow endearing stubbornness in the penultimate scene when she wanted to give Oathkeeper back to Jaime after the fulfilment of her mission.

She would never have thought of keeping the sword beyond the agreed time in her view or to act as though she had misunderstood Jaime in relation to the whereabouts of the Valyrian steel. This would go against all of her knightly principles. What would a spoken word be worth if you would not keep it or be judged by it?

The Blackfish, though, has no intention of escaping the castle together with Brienne and Podrick and simply giving up his family seat. Even though he knows that the stronghold has already been lost and his decision would mean certain death for him.

"Your family is in the North. Come with us. Don't die for pride when you can fight for your blood."
- **Brienne to Brynden Tully**

Even Brienne's urgent request not to sacrifice his life out of a false sense of honor but rather to help his remaining family in the North with his experience cannot change Sansa's great uncle's mind. Nevertheless, these words from the blonde woman seem to obviously impress the old man, and he now recognizes her noble character influenced by knightly virtues and how valuable Brienne could be for his grandniece in the future ("You'll serve her far better than I ever could."). It seems as if he sees a piece of himself from in her, when he was a younger man and full of energy, at this moment.

In contrast to the scene when Olenna Tyrell praised Brienne beyond all measure for her tournament victory against her grandson Loras (Episode 4.01 *Two Swords*) and she showed enormous difficulties in coping with it, Brienne is touched and moved in this moment, but a hint of pride can be seen in her facial expression to hear such words from a "legend", as Ser Davos recently called Sansa's great uncle at their briefing (Episode 6.05 *The Door*).

In fact, a nicer compliment could not be given to the Lady of Tarth...

This emotional farewell scene is abruptly interrupted by the suddenly approaching voices of his own men, clearly searching for the Blackfish.

When he heroically heads towards the noise with his sword drawn to bravely confront his opponents, despite the hopelessness of the situation, Brienne looks back at him for some time before making her way to Podrick in the prepared boat.

In this brief moment when she looks back at him, it is clear that the courage, determination and principled stance of the Blackfish make a lasting impression on her. What's more, despite all of the wistfulness, it fills her with joy to have finally met this man that essentially embodies all of the virtues (yes, including her extreme stubbornness) that she also values.

She can absolutely understand his way of thinking. After all, she was in a very similar mindset after Renly's murder when only Catelyn Stark's encouraging words kept her from senselessly giving her own life for a dead man.

As painful as the probable fate of the Blackfish may be, his fearless course of action gives Brienne and Podrick a little time to escape.

Location:
Riverrun, Riverlands

While all of the leaping trout banners of the Tullys are taken down in the castle and replaced by the lion of House Lannister and the twin towers of House Frey, Jaime receives news from one of his soldiers that the Blackfish was found, but died in the fighting. Jaime is almost motionless when he takes note of this fact, which must have left a sour taste in his mouth since it puts a slight damper on his triumph.

He would have loved to have rubbed his defeated opponent's nose in his ultimately futile stubbornness. And attentive viewers will know how such dialogues with the Kingslayer usually end up.

When Jaime gazes over the parapet of the castle wall shortly thereafter, gently rippling water draws his attention to a small rowboat slowly moving along the river away from the fortress. He immediately scraps the idea of calling his men and having the boat stopped when he realizes who the absconders most likely are: Brienne and Podrick.

A second, closer look then finally confirms his assumption when the woman turns to him.

Of course, it would have been easy for him to have his men chase and capture the pair. After all, the evaders make slow progress with the boat and the river is not too great an obstacle in this respect due to its width.

However, the Kingslayer instead hesitantly raises his hand to say farewell, which Brienne reciprocates just as tentatively before turning away from him again.

While Jaime finally allows the woman and her companion to escape into the cover of darkness, she looks into an uncertain future with an anxious facial expression.

Like the farewells from Harrenhal (Episode 3.07 *The Bear and the Maiden Fair*) and King's Landing (Episode 4.04 *Oathkeeper*), this separation scene between the two also has an air of melancholy and sadness without the use of a single word.

This scene also shows the viewer how much the two protagonists feel for each other and how this relationship is characterized by mutual respect and admiration for the other person.

Despite knowing that he and Brienne are on different political sides, he ultimately allows the woman, who means so much to him, to go and he also enables this without him or her losing face from this unpleasant affair. I like to call this an "escape route for heroes"...

Brienne's storyline ends unexpectedly early in the eighth episode of this season with her escape from Riverrun. In contrast, she always appeared in the respective final episodes of seasons two to five.
It will be interesting to see where her path will lead her.

Back to Sansa and her half-brother Jon, who finally managed to free Winterfell from the hands of Ramsay Bolton, and who had to pay dearly with the death of their brother Rickon? Or will she run into an old acquaintance, the Hound, who is now back in the world of the living, and who is also currently located in the Riverlands and only recently (back) in the company of the Brotherhood without Banners after his refuge in the form of the small church community was brutally taken away? Or will she reencounter Arya Stark, who is now on a revenge campaign against all those who virtually eradicated her family after returning from Braavos and her incomplete training to become an assassin, and who has already been able to mark a prominent victim, Walder Frey, off her list? We will know more in just over four months...

A Review of Season Six

While Brienne was mainly occupied with watching a certain window and waiting for an agreed signal in the second half of the previous season, the sixth season offers, in my view, the greatest variety of exciting, moving and (one may find it hard to believe in relation to Brienne) funny moments from her entire storyline so far.

The dramatically staged and successful rescue mission right at the beginning of the season is then followed by my personal favourite scene from her entire storyline so far, which can essentially be described in just one word: redemption. Brienne's kneel and oath of allegiance to Sansa Stark, and her expressed willingness to finally accept the steadfast and courageous woman into her service in return, is truly great emotional cinema.

In addition to the moment in season five when Brienne entrusts Podrick with her tragic past, this is the second scene within her storyline that repeatedly brings tears to my eyes.

Up to now, we have seen almost everything in Brienne's plotline. From dramatic sequences to tragic and heart-warming moments. But funny moments? No chance. This is due to the nature of things, in other words: Brienne herself.

It certainly could not have been expected that the Lady of Tarth would play a supporting role in one of the funniest scenes in the entire series. The tall woman did not enjoy her meeting with Tormund Giantsbane, unlike me and probably the majority of viewers, when the Wildling leader makes eyes at her at every opportunity and thus embarrasses her time and time again.

Her irritated looks in response to the Wildling's allusions are simply exquisite and the interactions between these two characters caused quite a furor on the internet.

Then, finally, there is the long-awaited reunion between Brienne and Jaime.

This meeting is not quite as harmonious as expected since the two are now on opposing sides leaving the audience somewhat unsatisfied. In the end, it is primarily Jaime's feelings for Brienne that allow the woman to escape.

Incidentally, I found Brienne's conversation with the Blackfish during the whole Riverrun plot to be particularly revealing.

Although he proves to be a stubborn negotiating partner, as Jaime had already predicted, the old man recognizes and admires Brienne's noble spirit in a very short time. It's a shame that there are not more people like him...

Character profiles
– missing or superfluous?

The profiles of all the characters with whom Brienne has personal or indirect contact over the course of her current five seasons should actually be presented at this point and on the following pages. But, as you can see, there is nothing here – apart from this text.

I truly thought long and hard about whether it is really necessary to once again go through the backgrounds of all the relevant characters here but I decided against it in the end. I think that the subject matter of this book is very specific and thus rather unsuitable for "newcomers". In my opinion, it does not make sense to read a book about Brienne of Tarth if you are not acquainted with the TV series or George R.R. Martin's novel series, and consequently do not know the character.
I therefore assume that all those who are interested in Brienne and her story are at least familiar with all of the characters in this book to some extent.
Furthermore, in my opinion, character descriptions would just unnecessarily inflate the book, depending on the level of detail.

For those who want to know more about the characters in this book, I very much recommend some excellent secondary literature. For example, *The Noble Houses of Westeros (Seasons 1–5)* published by the Panini publishing house or *Inside HBO's Game of Thrones (Seasons 1 & 2* and *3 & 4)*. Having said that, I have also specified a few less expensive options under the heading "My Web Link Recommendations" (page 255).

The Implementation of an Idea

When I decided at the end of 2015 to write a book about my favorite character from *Game of Thrones*, I was well aware of the fact that both the character Brienne of Tarth and the actress Gwendoline Christie enjoy a much higher degree of popularity and recognition in English-speaking regions than is the case in Germany and that accordingly the response would only be relatively modest.

That alone would be reason enough to publish the book in the English language. But, in my view, it only makes sense to translate a German text into English if you are a native English speaker yourself or if you engage in the services of one, and unfortunately this is almost prohibitively expensive for mere mortals.

However, since my desire to dedicate a book to this fascinating character and her likeable actress – no matter whether in German or English – and to bring it to like-minded people was far stronger and more important than the question of whether all my efforts are lucrative for me or not it did not require any further deliberation on my part. Had the financial aspect been of the utmost importance for me, I would have had to make this book about a character from this story who is significantly more popular in Germany. But then something absolutely crucial would have been missing on my part: PASSION.

Another advantage of a book publication in English would have been that I could have used all the wonderful original proper names, such as King's Landing, The Dreadfort or Moat Cailin, instead of having to resort to the slightly harsh-sounding German versions, such as Königsmund, Grauenstein or Maidengraben. This is a self-imposed assumption since I do not think much of using the original English names in a book written in the German language just because it sounds "more stylish" or "cooler", as they say. But this is just my very personal opinion.

The will was already there and, like probably all those who once were or still are active in literature, I faced the question of what I wanted to express in terms of content with this book and, above all, how I can reach readers and generate interest. Or to put it simply: I needed a concept.

I finally came to the idea of separating Brienne's storyline from the overall *Game of Thrones* construct and then put this together scene by scene so that the result is an independent and coherent story at the end. This approach might be particularly interesting primarily for all those who, like me, favor a very specific character in the series. All other story lines are only addressed as required, and there is no need to skip over past other characters before returning to a Brienne scene, like in Martin's books with its various POV* chapters.

---

*[Point of view] a book chapter from the narrative perspective from a certain character

---

I was aware that a simple retelling or summary of her story so far would not necessarily offer major added value to the reader. So, I took each scene individually, summarized them and supplemented them with distinctive quotes and my own interpretation of what we have seen.

My goal: to trace Brienne's behavior and development scene by scene and episode by episode in as much detail as possible and to discuss this with my own thoughts and ideas.

Of course, one's own interpretations are always subjective. However, in my view, the attraction here lies in looking at the behavior analytically from the perspective of a fan without necessarily having to comply with the intentions of the screenwriters or the director.

In this respect, events that take place far away from Brienne's plot and consequently initially have no relevance to her story, but then subsequently affect her fate, posed a very specific hurdle. For example, the Red Wedding, the Battle of the Blackwater or the murder of Lysa Arryn.

It was a rather difficult balancing act at times that had to be mastered. The incorporation of retrospectives and explanations should therefore serve to provide a better understanding of the complex connections.

In order to provide background information for viewers, who were unaware as to how and why the whole Brienne plot got rolling, I included a short review of the significant events for Brienne's storyline from the first season and the first two episodes of the second season before the actual core of the book.

The most important background information regarding the character of Brienne and of course also Gwendoline Christie, i.e. the woman who was essentially the crucial factor in me making this project a reality, should give you the opportunity to take a look behind the facade of the character and the actress at the beginning of the book. After all, you should know what to expect...

For the conclusion, I then referred to topics I had dealt with for some time and that I considered to be worthy of mention and discussion. For example, the differences between "Show Brienne" and "Book Brienne" or the various accusations that were spreading throughout internet forums in relation to her character.

And then I went and did it after all...

This chapter must seem a bit bizarre to you, right? Even though I ruled out the publication of my book in the English language for financial reasons at the beginning of this section, you are now holding a copy – in English. There is a very simple explanation:

As previously mentioned, for several years, actress and series character have been becoming increasingly popular, particularly in the United Kingdom, that cannot be overlooked. I therefore considered the pros and cons of a translation once again and I decided to go for it, despite the financial cost. It would be a real shame to deprive this loyal fan base of such a book simply because it was written in the "wrong" language.

The Visual Compromise

After it became known in mid-2011 that Gwendoline Christie would take on the role of Brienne of Tarth in the second season of *Game of Thrones*, there were a number of fans of the book series who deemed her to be "too pretty". Even the actress herself found this statement "amazing" (source: ew.com) since she had already encountered a lot of adjectives regarding her appearance, but they did not include "too pretty".

Yet, George R.R. Martin, the author of the fantasy saga, was fascinated and impressed by the audition and appearance of the previously unknown British stage actress to such an extent that he wanted to reassure all those who feared a miscast in his blog at grrm.livejournal.com:

"This was another one of those cases where there was hardly any debate. The day the first batch of auditions went up for the role, we looked at a dozen actresses who were reading for Brienne and one actress who WAS Brienne. Gwendoline gave a great reading, and her look was just perfect. (…) She came in looking... well, like Brienne."

After all, he must know best since he created Brienne himself and thus he must have had a fairly clear picture of what this character should look like.

However, by taking a look at Martin's description of the Maiden of Tarth in his books, some of the grumbling from individual book readers regarding the choice of actress appears to be somehow understandable in hindsight:

"Beauty, they called her... mocking. The hair beneath the visor was a squirrel's nest of dirty straw, and her face... Brienne's eyes were large and very blue, a young girl's eyes, trusting and guileless, but the rest... her features were

broad coarse, her teeth prominent and crooked, her mouth too wide and her lips so plump, they seemed swollen. A thousand freckles speckled her cheeks and brow, and her nose had been broken more than once."
("A Song of Ice and Fire", Book 2: "A Clash of Kings", page 344)

With regard to an existing novel character, there is always the problem that the book reader has an image of this character in their head, and they obviously want to see this image realized accordingly when the book is filmed. This is certainly no different for the character of Brienne of Tarth. Since I had not yet read the books by Brienne's first appearance in the second season, as previously mentioned, I was unable to compare Brienne's book description with her appearance in the TV adaptation at that time. I then took this opportunity much, much later. To be more precise, during between the broadcasts of the fourth and fifth seasons.

Of course, I can only speak for myself, but I must admit that I am really grateful that the series creators did not explicitly abide by the book template in relation to the character of Brienne and I think that I am not alone with this opinion.
I think that the solution that was found regarding her appearance is a complete success. She has still kept her flaxen hair, her bitter, masculine face and her blue eyes from the books... oh yes, I almost forgot the all-important feature: fortunately, Ms. Christie is also the required size.
In my opinion, the make-up artists fully succeeded in making Brienne look as graceless and unwomanly as possible, without disfiguring her in a step towards the Uruk-hai from *Lord of the Rings*.

Of Heroes, Gods and
and Championed Causes

With Brienne, George R.R. Martin created a character who well and truly stirs up or turns the traditional distribution of roles between males and females and the paradigm of the strong and weak gender upside down.

Of course, this characterization gives us plenty to talk about and it appears that not everyone has unconditional goodwill for her. At least, this is my impression when I occasionally visit various German or English language *GoT* forums.

Granted, there are fans of the series who do not have any particular sympathy for my favorite character, or who even find her annoying or superfluous. After all, there are even one or two characters in the *GoT* universe that I do not think much of.

Nevertheless, is it necessary to wish for a character, who is one of the most loyal, honorable and reliable characters in the story, to be killed off next? Why is Brienne often accused of being a so-called "Mary-Sue"[1], a "Dea ex machina"[2] or simply extremely fortunate to be alive in misogynistic posts? I will attempt to answer these questions on the following pages.

---

[1] A fan fiction synonym for a female character who is exceptionally pretty and/or has outstanding abilities, has (virtually) no faults and easily defies all opposition due to her talent. "Mary-Sue" has its origins in a *Star Trek* parody published by Paula Smith in 1974 under the title *A Trekkie's Tale*. The author introduced a new, self-created character with the female lieutenant Mary-Sue - half-human, half-Vulcan. With her idealized and extraordinary abilities, she heroically saves the lives of Kirk, Spock and Dr. McCoy but sacrifices her own life in turn.

A common expression nowadays for a "last-minute rescue" from an almost hopeless situation by an event or person, for which there is no rational justification and which are generally referred to as "miracles" or divine intervention.

In the ancient world of theater, primarily in Greek tragedies, the "deus/dea ex machina" [lat. "God/Goddess from a machine"] was often used to resolve a hopeless conflict towards the end of the piece where a deity would be lowered to the stage using a crane-like machine.

A character without faults or flaws

In today's modern age, there still seems to be many men of this world who see characters like Brienne as a threat to the male status quo, and who obviously have problems with changes to existing stereotypes that are unalterable for them.

Even the first assertion that Brienne is a "Mary-Sue", i.e. a fictional and, by definition, not only beautiful, but also absolutely flawless and almost invincible character in every respect, brings a smirk to my face while I am writing these lines.

There is no doubt that Brienne knows how to handle a sword excellently. However, that is where the parallels end since, in my view, this theory does not hold up for all the other comparisons. Although she has been able to win every duel so far, I personally never thought to describe her as invincible in the same way as a "Terminator" because she simply had to take too much damage in most of her duels. Fortunately, she is just human and not a "Supergirl" transported to the middle ages by Warner Studios with a big "S" on her chest who defies the force of gravity and successively renders her enemies harmless with her supernatural abilities. Perhaps it is just a matter of time until she meets an opponent who is better than her. Hold on! No... she had better not.

I certainly cannot understand the other Mary-Sue aspect of having little or no weaknesses in relation to Brienne. In this respect, her shortcomings when encountering other people are simply too blatant - just think of the way she treated Podrick for a long time - and her actions are rarely based on clever reasoning.

The best examples of this are her behavior after Renly Baratheon's murder when she did not want to leave the dead man's side (Episode 2.05 *The Ghost of Harrenhal*) or when she innocently approached Littlefinger's table at the inn in the Vale of Arryn and thus put herself in grave danger (Episode 5.02 *The House of Black and White*). Although these actions are typical for the character of Brienne, they clearly disqualify her as an almost perfect character in the sense of a "Mary-Sue".

I have also already dealt with the topic of Brienne and appearance in great detail in the chapter "The Visual Compromise"... In my opinion, more words are not needed.

Goddess from a machine

The next point of criticism that Brienne is a "Dea ex machina" or – as I read in multiple forums – a "Dea ex Brienne", a savior, a heroine, who always suddenly appears on the scene to help other characters from life threatening emergencies at the last minute, is no less remarkable.

I could watch all of the Brienne scenes countless times and my opinion would not change. I refer back to only two scenes in her entire plot where it could be suggested that Brienne could possibly possess this "savior" gene. And even this seems rather poorly construed in both cases: The first example can be seen in episode 5.02 *The House of Black and White* when Brienne rescues Podrick from the knights of the Vale of Arryn at the end, as well as in episode 6.01 *The Red Woman*, when she and her squire free Sansa and Theon from the Bolton men. In my view, these are sequences that I have already discussed in detail in the specified sections where I explained and put the "Dea ex machina" character into perspective in the given circumstances.

These Brienne scenes sparkle with plausibility in comparison to one of the most famous and probably most striking "Deus-ex-machina" moments in film history, the unexpected rescue of the main character by an alien space ship in the Monty Python classic *Life of Brian* (1979), or – and I have difficulty in admitting this – the somehow always foreseeable rescues of my childhood heroes in the various Karl May films of the 1960s (Sorry, Lex!).

Furthermore, if we take a look at other storylines in the series, the sudden appearance of the knights of the Vale of Arryn and thus the accompanying rescue of Jon Snow's clearly outnumbered allies in the battle for Winterfell in *Battle of the Bastards* (Episode 6.09) could just as well be described as a "Dei ex machina" moment as the surprising arrival of the Lannister army at the Battle of the Blackwater (Episode 2.09 *Blackwater*). Furthermore, the life-saving arrival of Stannis Baratheon's forces at the Wall, when the Night's Watch was threatened with being overrun by the Wildlings (Episode 4.09 *The Watchers on the Wall*) provides another instance. These are all scenes that are almost identical to one of the key moments in the second part of the *Lord of the Rings* trilogy, *The Two Towers*, when Gandalf and the Riders of Rohan ultimately, decisively intervene in the Battle for Helms Deep, which was almost entirely lost. In this respect, there are not only ample similar examples but also much more characteristic examples both inside and outside of the series. And this list could easily be continued

However, I am not aware of that there were ever any public criticisms of these resolutions.

How great would the outcry have been on the various internet platforms if Brienne and Podrick had not saved Sansa and Theon from their pursuers? Brienne especially would have been accused of incompetence. After all, she was nearby and she would have heard the loud dog barking. It is a lose-lose situation. Unfortunately, you cannot please everyone.

Brienne, the lucky one

I find the last topic, the accusation that Brienne's survival in the series so far is based solely on luck and less due to her exceptional talent of handling a sword, her patience or her perseverance, particularly... well, sort of "bold".

I do not want to get too philosophical with regards to the definition of the word "luck". On the one hand, this would be going too far and, alternatively, I would rather leave this to people who deal with it professionally and thus have a much better knowledge of the subject than me. Nevertheless, in order to deal with this topic reasonably as a layperson, one should at least know that luck can be divided into two categories: "luck", commonly referred to as "being lucky", and "happiness", usually seen as the result of a lengthier process. Even though the latter form of luck is not a point of criticism, I would now like to take a closer look at it in relation to Brienne. If the topic of "luck" is already being edited, why not do it correctly?

In my view, mentioning Brienne and luck (in the sense of perceived happiness) in the same breath bears comparison to a Biathlon World Championship in the Bahamas or a barrier-free prison cell – an oxymoron.
Of course, there are happy, hopeful and beautiful moments in Brienne's life. In most cases, these moments are

promptly ruined by a stroke of fate or a decision she is not responsible for.

I am talking about a situation, a tragedy that virtually began with her introduction to the series when she finally fulfilled her dream of becoming a member of Renly's Kingsguard only to have to witness his assassination shortly thereafter, weaving a mark on her storyline like a common thread ever since.

Even though all of the subsequent events where this stereotypical interdependence emerges do not involve murder or death – in which case she would have to seriously consider therapeutic treatment –, they once again illustrate how joy and sorrow, confidence and despair appear to be inseparable in relation to Brienne's storyline.

A prime example of this can be seen in Episode 5.03 (*High Sparrow*) when Brienne reveals her sad story to Podrick and she utters the word "happy" in relation to herself for the first and only time. Despite the search for suitors arranged by her father that he had to force her to attend, she had "never been so happy". This was the case up to the moment when, to her disappointment, she discovered that the flattery from all the suitors present was just an act and she was secretly being mocked.

What is particularly striking about this topic is that all of the encounters that she eagerly awaited actually ended in major disappointment for her, such as the sudden and unexpected meeting with Arya Stark (Episode 4.10 *The Children*), who she was looking for, and the encounter with her sister Sansa shortly thereafter (Episode 5.02 *The House of Black and White*) as well as her chance reunion with Jaime Lannister (Episode 6.08 *No One*).

With regards to the two Stark sisters, she thought that she could keep her once sworn oath, only to be abruptly rejected each time by the two young women.

As for Jaime, it was primarily the events surrounding the siege of Riverrun and the sorrowful realization that they are standing and, if necessary, fighting on different sides, which threw an obstacle in her plan to enjoy her brief meeting with him.

This lively emotional roller coaster ride can also include her subsequent negotiation with the Blackfish (Episode 6.08 *No One*) or her brief conversation with Cersei Lannister at Joffrey's wedding ceremony (Episode 4.02 *The Lion and the Rose*).

While Brienne was visibly glad to finally persuade the old man to listen to her concerns, the hope of successfully fulfilling her mission was immediately destroyed when he eventually denied her his support for personal reasons.

The situation with Jaime's twin sister is very similar. The initial praise for Brienne having brought her brother to the capital was followed by a verbal foot sweep when Cersei accused Brienne of throwing herself at whoever suits her and falling in love with Jaime.

In the latter case, Brienne's facial expression is beautifully illustrated by the initial embarrassed joy up to complete bewilderment.

Even the two moments when Brienne swore her loyalty to Catelyn Stark (Episode 2.05 *The Ghost of Harrenhal*) and then later to her daughter Sansa (Episode 6.01 *The Red Woman*), and she saw the goal of her dreams, these did not really make her happy in retrospect since both mother and daughter sent her on missions shortly thereafter. Both women renounced her personal protection and thus reduced Brienne's actual intention to absurdity. She had certainly not imagined that "protection" would entail escorting Jaime Lannister or struggling away with the Blackfish. In this respect, her disappointment in Sansa's case is absolutely understandable.

Brienne probably saw the Stark daughter as the person who urgently needed her protection based on what had happened to her so far. And then this person sent her, Brienne, away.

When thinking back to her tearful and hopeful look at the moment when she was taken into the service of the Stark girl, and the fact that she repeatedly put her life at risk for this purpose, one can feel how much it must have hurt her.

In my opinion, there are only three situations over the course of her five-season storyline where the viewer sees a truly happy and content Brienne without the rug being instantly pulled out from under her feet.

Firstly, there is an example in episode 4.04 (*Oathkeeper*), when Jaime gives her the Valyrian steel sword and new armor. This situation completely overwhelms her, she is full of emotions and does not know how to deal with it.

Secondly, another example is in episodes 5.03 and 6.08 (*High Sparrow* and *No One*) when both Podrick and the Blackfish give her words of praise and respect. On the one hand, for her victorious duel with the Hound and, on the other, full of admiration for her loyal attitude. These two also managed to bring tears of emotion to Brienne's eyes with their remarks. But I would still not describe them as a lucky streak...

The fact that Brienne, unlike the viewer, never knew retrospectively, and never will know, that she missed Sansa twice by a hair's breadth when she was searching for her (Episodes 5.01 and 5.10 *The Wars to Come* and *Mother's Mercy*), can also be viewed as a certain form of luck, so to speak. After all, this lack of knowledge keeps her from completely sinking into self-pity and feeling like the most useless person in the world.

Brienne, favored by luck

"She has always been lucky!"
This is sometimes the succinct answer you get if you ask fans of the series who do not think much of the Lady of Tarth and why they consider this the reason that Brienne is still alive. But is it actually so simple?

Brienne's exceptional abilities in handling a sword and her physical condition undoubtedly form an almost perfect combination that is difficult to crack. The two Kingsguards that mistakenly deemed her to be Renly's murderer in episode 2.05 (*The Ghost of Harrenhal*) and immediately attacked her, were the first to be painfully convinced that her victory against Loras Tyrell was no accident.

The same applies for the Hound, who she was ultimately able to defeat in a merciless duel in Episode 4.10 *The Children*. She also won duels against the knights of the Vale of Arryn in episode 5.02 *The House of Black and White* as well as the Bolton men in episode 6.01 *The Red Woman*. Brienne became the undoing for all of them, except for the Hound who, as we now know, was eventually saved.

I personally do not believe that it is so extraordinary that Brienne has this gift as a woman. It was not long ago that author George R.R. Martin first confirmed that she is a descendent of Ser Duncan the Tall, one of the most famous knights of Westeros and former Lord Commander of the Kingsguard, and thus she may well have inherited his genes. The flashback with Ser Arthur Dayne, a former member of Aerys II. Targaryen's Kingsguard in episode 6.03 (*Oathbreaker*) shows that one can take on multiple opponents with enough talent. Why not her, too?

Perhaps only her victory against the Hound could be attributed to the fact that he suffered an infection from a bite wound (during another storyline) shortly before their momentous encounter and thus he may have been a little groggy. However, as a viewer, I did not notice any impairment during the fight.

Even if Sandor Clegane was one hundred percent fit on that day, he most likely would have struggled against the furious Brienne.

Perhaps he would have defeated her. Perhaps not.

During Brienne's encounter with the three Northmen (Episode 2.10 *Valar morghulis*), in addition to her repeatedly mentioned physique and talent, another aspect has a crucial role to play in their ultimate fate: the fatal error of not seeing her as an equal opponent, seemingly also relying on numerical superiority. The Kingslayer, Jaime Lannister, also made this mistake.

Despite months of captivity, chains and the fact that he was a little out of practice, he was absolutely certain that Brienne would not constitute a major obstacle for one of the most gifted swordsmen in Westeros when he was able to steal the second sword from her and instigated a small duel on the bridge (Episode 3.02 *Dark Wings, Dark Words*). The result is well known.

Accordingly, his own arrogance, disregard for his opponent and Brienne's abilities in handling a sword were the main reasons for her survival, at least in these two cases. But is it really her problem if people do not take her seriously? Probably not.

In my view, none of the specified situations can be unreservedly categorized as "lucky". Even the scene with the Hound cannot disprove this.

If at all, in relation to Brienne, so-called "luck" in just two scenes in the third season can be used as a reason for her survival in the series - and Jaime Lannister plays a significant role in both cases: on the one hand, when he saves her from the threat of rape (and perhaps even worse) by the Bolton men (Episode 3.03 *Walk of Punishment*) with an invented story and, on the other, when he selflessly rescues her from a bear pit (Episode 3.07 *The Bear and the Maiden Fair*).

Of course, at first glance, Brienne was "lucky" both times since she would have been hopelessly lost without Jaime's intervention. However, if we dig a little deeper, then there are quite plausible reasons for his actions that I have already addressed in the corresponding chapters. These reasons are based on hypotheses and cannot be completely proven, as mentioned. The screenwriters could certainly make a more specific statement in this respect...

I think that I have made one thing very clear with my remarks:
Brienne has not had much "happiness" or "luck" but rather the contrary. In my view, she is still one of the unluckiest surviving characters in the story

This seems even more obvious if, for example, you look at Tyrion Lannister's storyline.
He has been saved from five life-threatening situations so far: by Bronn at a judgement by the Gods at the Eyrie (Episode 1.06 *A Golden Crown*), by his squire Podrick during the Battle of the Blackwater (Episode 2.09 *Blackwater*) and by his brother Jaime, who freed him from his cell after a lost trial by combat and thus saved him from execution (Episode 4.10 *The Children*). Tyrion also owed his life to Jorah Mormont twice within a short period of time in episode 5.05 (*Kill the Boy*): first, when he saves him from the

"stone men" and then from drowning immediately after. That's right, life can sometimes be quite unjust...

And finally, my question: viewed objectively, can Brienne still be accused of being a "lucky devil" and leading a charmed life?

Angela Wiederhut
Brienne's German voice

When it comes to films or TV series, there is nothing more distracting than mistimed voice-overs.

In my opinion, however, the selection of 40-year-old Munich-born Angela Wiederhut as the voice actress of Brienne of Tarth was a very good decision. I find her voice to be truly pleasant and absolutely authentic for the character of Brienne.

Even in *The Hunger Games: Mockingjay, Part 2* (Christie as "Commander Lyme") and *Absolutely Fabulous: The Movie* (Christie as herself), Angela Wiederhut can be heard as the "German version" of the Brit, as it were.

For the dubbing of "Captain Phasma" in *Star Wars: Episode VII – The Force Awakens*, though, FFS Film- & Fernseh-Synchron GmbH hired Wiederhut's colleague Katrin Fröhlich. A change that I was a little irritated by since I had become very accustomed with Ms. Wiederhut as Christie's German voice for a couple of years.

Although I have now come to terms with this, I was still curious about how this change of voice artist, which was unnecessary from my view, came about. So, I asked Ms. Wiederhut herself. Her response came promptly and she informed me that FFS never invited her to a voice casting for this role. In this respect, in her own words, she would have very happily performed the voice-over for this role and her schedule would have been clear for it.

Perhaps the dubbing studio thought that her voice was simply unsuitable for this specific character, but this is merely a presumption on her part.

We will probably never know the real reasons.

Ms. Wiederhut can already look back upon numerous engagements as a voice actress, and I would wager that her voice will be familiar to one or more readers from other film or TV productions. However, it would go beyond the scope to list her entire filmography here.

If you want to find out more about Angela Wiederhut and her speaking roles, then have a look at the following German websites:

www.angelawiederhut.de and **www.synchronkartei.de**

My Web Link Recommendations

- **gwendoline-christie.com [Glorious Gwendoline Christie]**
THE (unofficial) website where just about everything interesting and worth-knowing about Gwendoline Christie can be seen and read.
In addition to biographical facts on the actress, this web site has countless photos, screenshots, videos and interviews, not just regarding "Brienne" or "Game of Thrones" in general, but also regarding her other projects, e.g. "Star Wars".

- **www.facebook.com/Gwendoline-Christie**
Gwendoline Christie's Facebook account

- **twitter.com/lovegwendoline [@lovegwendoline]**
Gwendoline Christie's Twitter account

- **jaimebrienne.com [Jaime & Brienne Online]**
A forum which almost exclusively deals with the relationship (incl. fan fiction) between Jaime and Brienne.

- **gameofthrones.wikia.com/wiki/Game_of_Thrones_Wiki**
General databases for the TV series "Game of Thrones". Here you can find out everything about the characters. There is also an episode guide.

- **watchersonthewall.com**
- **winteriscoming.com**
Websites that contain news, rumors, casting information and speculation about "Game of Thrones".

- **imdb.com**
General database with forum (message board) regarding "Game of Thrones".

- **quartermaster.info**
Interactive map which can be used to (almost) precisely track the routes of selected characters from both the book series and the TV series

Screenshot references (pages 26 – 231):

Game of Thrones – Season 2 (DVD, Production: HBO, Distribution: Warner Home Video Germany, 2012), episodes used: 2.03, 2.04, 2.05, 2.06, 2.07, 2.08, 2.10

Game of Thrones – Season 3 (DVD, Production: HBO, Distribution: Warner Home Video Germany, 2013), episodes used: 3.02, 3.03, 3.04, 3.05, 3.06, 3.07, 3.10

Game of Thrones – Season 4 (DVD, Production: HBO, Distribution: Warner Home Video Germany, 2014), episodes used: 4.01, 4.02, 4.03, 4.04, 4.05, 4.07, 4.10

Game of Thrones – Season 5 (DVD, Production: HBO, Distribution: Warner Home Video Germany, 2015), episodes used: 5.01, 5.02, 5.03, 5.04, 5.05, 5.07, 5.10

Game of Thrones – Season 6 (DVD, Production: HBO, Distribution: Warner Home Video Germany, 2016), episodes used: 6.01, 6.02, 6.04, 6.05, 6.07, 6.08

Quote references (pages 24 – 231):

Game of Thrones – Season 1 (DVD, Production: HBO, Distribution: Warner Home Video Germany, 2011), episode used: 1.07

Game of Thrones – Season 2 (DVD, Production: HBO, Distribution: Warner Home Video Germany, 2012), episodes used: 2.03, 2.04, 2.05, 2.06, 2.07, 2.08, 2.10

Game of Thrones – Season 3 (DVD, Production: HBO, Distribution: Warner Home Video Germany, 2013), episodes used: 3.02, 3.03, 3.04, 3.05, 3.06, 3.07, 3.10

Game of Thrones – Season 4 (DVD, Production: HBO, Distribution: Warner Home Video Germany, 2014), episodes used: 4.01, 4.02, 4.03, 4.04, 4.05, 4.07, 4.10

Game of Thrones – Season 5 (DVD, Production: HBO, Distribution: Warner Home Video Germany, 2015), episodes used: 5.01, 5.02, 5.03, 5.04, 5.05, 5.07, 5.10

Game of Thrones – Season 6 (DVD, Production: HBO, Distribution: Warner Home Video Germany, 2016), episodes used: 6.01, 6.02, 6.04, 6.05, 6.07, 6.08

References for biographical information:

All the information mentioned in the "Phoenix from the Ashes" chapter (pages 11 – 22) regarding Gwendoline Christie's acting career was taken from the internet portals specified under "My Web Link Recommendations". In order to ensure the reproduction was as accurate as possible, I referred to a multitude of information from several sources at the same time for the purpose of comparison.

Other sources: quartermaster.info

This website served to determine the sometimes rather vague location information more precisely.

German language quotes:

All of the German language quotes used in this book that were translated into English have been professionally translated by a native speaker. The same applies for the quotes on the back of the book.

What I wanted to get off my chest at the end:

In truth, it still seems surreal to me. I actually managed to not only write my first book but also get it published.
Until a few years ago, I could never have dreamt of this achievement.
I found reading books to be extremely boring. So, why would I ever have the idea to write one? Simply absurd. Whenever there was the opportunity, I preferred to watch the film adaptation. This was the case for "Lord of the Rings" and "Harry Potter". Above all, it was much easier and faster. Previously, I only voluntarily read the current TV guide. Or at the hairdressers. Or in the doctors' waiting room. But, of course, only to not fall asleep or just to "kill" time, and not because the various magazines contained insanely exciting articles.
It may well be that this former aversion to books came from my school days. In contrast to my favourite subjects, English and Latin, I downright hated German language lessons. In particular, for me, essays were always like desperate attempts to scale the north face of the Eiger and thus usually ended in fiasco.
Thankfully, habits and views change over the course of a lifetime. I have now read "Lord of the Rings" and "Harry Potter" - and I have my first own book on the shelf. I would therefore like to express my warmest thanks to two dear people:

I would like to thank my wife, who agreed to check my book for spelling and grammar in advance, even though I often drove her up the wall with my writings. Without her help, the correct formulation of "conspired" would probably still be in the incorrect past participle form in the review on page 100. Her initial skepticism regarding my writing

style and the content was followed by very positive feedback after just a few pages ("I hate to admit it, but it makes very exciting reading.").
Thank you very much! It means a lot to me!

My thanks also go to Philipp-M. Wegner who designed the magnificent front cover based on my ideas. It was a real challenge to design Brienne so that the image resembles the series original but does not 100% match it due to German copyright law. It was also not easy to find an interested and motivated illustrator. My requests often went unanswered, or the initial interest suddenly disappeared when the artist wanted to know precisely which character from the series it concerned. Poor Brienne! That was not very nice. Therefore, I am more than pleased that Mr. Wegner is just as big a fan of the *Game of Thrones* series as I am and the creation of the cover image was "a small affair of the heart" for him, as he put it.
Thank you very much for the great cooperation and your patience with me

How did you like this book? Do you have any criticisms?
Feel free to write to me at

oathkeeper@gmx.de